Life runs efficiently when nothing hurts.

In Meiyu, people clip away their heaviest emotions and store them in memory drives so life can continue neatly and undisturbed. Lena is a courier who delivers these sealed fragments across the island, her days defined by routine, distance, and careful neutrality.

When one delivery goes wrong, a defective drive activates in her hands. The feelings inside are not hers, and they were never meant to surface. Ignoring protocol, Lena follows its pull through the city, through night markets scented with scallion and fried dough, into noodle shops and the quiet generosity of neighbors' kitchens, where lives brush against one another. With each step, the walls she's built around herself begin to thin.

All That Holds Between is a gentle speculative novella about rediscovering what's lost, savoring what remains, and allowing life to hold more than function.

ALL THAT HOLDS BETWEEN

ALSO BY S.J. LEE

The Altered Earth Trilogy
Of Friction
Of Abrasion
Of Imperfection

ALL THAT HOLDS BETWEEN

S.J. LEE

PEW BOOKS

Library of Congress Cataloging-in-Publication Data is available.

ISBN (paperback) 979-8-9892965-9-0
ISBN (ebook) 979-8-9892965-8-3

Cover illustration by Chia-Chi Yu (余嘉琪)
Cover design by S.J. Lee (李悅溢)
Interior illustrations by Stephany Lai (賴思妤)

ALL THAT HOLDS BETWEEN

HALCYON INTEGRATED WELLNESS PROMO
TELEVISION COMMERCIAL SCRIPT

[OPENING SHOT: MEIYU – EARLY MORNING]
Sunlight washes over the island harbor as bicycles weave down the main street into the waking city.

VOICEOVER (V.O.):
"In Meiyu, every day begins with possibility. And when life is unburdened, we move and live with ease."

[CUT TO: MEIYU DAY MONTAGE]
[EAST MARKET]
A breakfast stall vendor hands a steaming hot meal to an office worker. A grandmother selects fresh vegetables, and the vendor scans her wristband with a smile.
[MEIYU SUBWAY STATION]
A business executive taps his wristband and enters an express lane.
[HOSPITAL]

A parent holding a sleeping toddler sits in a priority
waiting room.
[COMMUNITY CENTER]
An elderly uncle steps into a tai chi class. A young couple
laughs in a calligraphy workshop nearby.

ON-SCREEN TEXT:
Meal Vouchers
Market Discounts
Transit Credits
Priority Access
Community Engagement

V.O.:
"With the Balance Treatment, Halcyon Wellness helps you
make room for the moments that matter. Gentle, guided
support for the emotions that drag you down—paired
with everyday partner benefits across the city. From meal
vouchers and market savings to priority access and
community opportunities, life flows effortlessly wherever
you go."

[CUT TO: VARIOUS RESIDENTS]
A teacher kneels beside a student, pointing at a line on
their tablet. A street cleaner waves at a child. A barista
holds out a drink with a smile.

V.O.:
"More time for what matters: family and loved ones,
work, and your health and wellbeing."

[CUT TO: HALCYON BALANCE CENTER]
A Restoration Practitioner welcomes a well-dressed couple with an easy smile.

V.O.:
"The Balance Treatment eases the weight.
And you stay you, simply with more space to breathe."

[CLOSING SHOT: MEIYU AT GOLDEN HOUR]
Bicycles glide home. Families gather for dinner in their spacious apartments. Laundry on a balcony sways in the breeze. The city glows.

V.O.:
"Halcyon Wellness. Feel lighter. Live steadier.
And let Meiyu shine with you."

ON-SCREEN TEXT:
HALCYON WELLNESS
Lighten the load. Lift the day.

ONE

Efficiency sets the pace of the world. And despite all the upgraded machines and advanced sciences, there's a stubborn dependability to a bicycle, its simple design unchanged year after year. No motor to service, no battery to charge, no software waiting to fail. Legs power the pedals, the chain turns, the wheels follow, and the outcome remains consistent. A bicycle is practical, durable, and inexpensive. Fast, but not *too* fast.

Efficiency in physical form. Lena likes that.

To her side, her reflection ripples on the glass. Wrapped in her hooded poncho, she appears more shape than person, a pinched triangle on two wheels. Most days she doesn't mind the ride, but she's more than ready for the sky to clear. Mountainous clouds squat over the island, and this morning's downpour has slackened into a drizzle that clings to Lena's cheeks. While she waits, she runs her thumb along the jagged groove of the handlebar where a small well of water has pooled. A prickle of irritation surfaces, although the old anger doesn't rise.

When the traffic signal shifts, she pushes off and glides toward the lower ring. Water threads the painted lines that run beside her tracks, and Lena doesn't bother with the street signs and markings. Routine and familiar motion carry her.

Ahead, a large white building emerges with HALCYON BALANCE CENTER across the front in bright signage. Moisture streaks down its wide panes, blurring the reception area on the other side. The clinic opens in twenty minutes, and already there's a modest queue forming due to the rainy weather, although it'll be nothing like the post-summer and holiday crowds. Her old office sits in the east wing beyond the interior service desk, likely reassigned the week she left. Maybe the demotion might have stung to someone else, *somewhere else*, but not Lena, and not on the island city of Meiyu.

Her pace quickens as she pedals by, although there's no reason to care if anyone glances out. None of her former coworkers would recognize her beneath the poncho, anyway. Plus, couriers rarely draw a second look, especially on a day like this.

At the exit to the lower road, traffic thickens. Reflective armbands catch the passing light from vehicles and storefront signs, and other handlebar lamps blink amber and red against the film of rain on asphalt. Lena keeps to the shoulder and takes the turn overlooking the harbor's edge. Cargo haulers drift in the distance.

The weather smothers most of the brine emanating

from the nearby fish market, but like every other day, Lena angles her face away. For someone who grew up surrounded by the sea, she's never cared for its taste (it's fine to admire, but not to eat). She passes compact stalls, their haze escaping from awnings and disappearing into the cool air. An electric truck drones by, its bulk momentarily crowding the lane, and she falls in behind a few cyclists skimming through gaps too narrow for anything larger. Through the mist, billboards glow.

HALCYON INTEGRATED WELLNESS
CALM HOUSEHOLDS,
STRONG NEIGHBORHOODS

A family of three smiles beneath a pastel gradient, their posture perfect. Serenity, all arranged. And below them, a smaller sign scrolls district clinic hours, queue durations, and the latest maintenance plans.

To her left, she passes a century-old station still in use. Beyond it, the tram slices through the island, rails gleaming as the cars climb toward the newer sections of the city. Lena stays on the lower level, where Old Meiyu keeps to its slower cadence. Here, buildings retain their first bones: sloped roofs, brick fronts, close-set balconies dotted with herbs and clotheslines, and alleys unchanged across generations.

She cuts across the causeway, and another courier moving in the opposite direction tips a hand her way. Lena doesn't know them, but she answers with a wave. It's simply an acknowledgment. Recognition isn't the point, nor is further engagement. Just like finding like.

At the next intersection, a municipal screen cycles through the week's forecast: light showers, shifting winds, variable conditions. In the corner, Halcyon's logo gleams beside its usual reminder about rebates for emotionally balanced citizens. Lena doesn't need to read the entire thing; no one does. It always repeats with the morning announcements, sandwiched between the same slogans: *Balance earns trust. Balance earns stability.*

The corporation city guides her along, one billboard after another, and the mantra trails her all the way to the Halcyon depot. The bay door lifts, and she rolls inside, greeted by warm air tinged with a blend of metal polish, burnt coffee, and a touch of ozone from the scanners. Overhead fluorescents replace the dimness outside. Old Man Hsieh sits at his security post with his dented thermos, shoulders rounded, eyes roving between the monitors and nothing in particular. A pile of sandbags rests nearby. Lena gives him a nod, and he returns it.

She parks her bicycle just inside the entrance, sheds her poncho and helmet, and shakes out her damp hair. She taps her armband against the check-in scanner and retrieves her handheld from the thin bag slung across her chest. Halcyon's application spools, and the route loads: one delivery to an office tower in the nicer strip, four deliveries in the interior business district near the research labs, one to her prior office address, and a last stop at Disposal. Plus any Halcyon errands that come along the way. It's not a terribly busy schedule. With a week of wet weather, she expected more volume.

Mr. Peng, Lena's middle-aged supervisor, steps out from the back office with a silicone-cased tablet balanced in one hand. He wears round gold spectacles, has a silver patch in his neatly combed hair, and moves with the precision of someone who dislikes wasted motion. Even though digital clocks blink around the space, he still checks the time on his analog wristwatch.

"Good morning, Ms. Li." Like his posture and motions, his voice is measured, never raised.

"Morning," she answers.

"Humidity's high today," he notes, glancing at the diagnostic strip behind Old Man Hsieh. "The older sleeves don't hold their seals well in this. Double-check the readings before you head out. Swap anything that runs high, and log the change."

"Understood."

"And routing checkpoints are lagging after the last system update. Add cushion where you can."

"Will do."

His gaze finds the bicycle behind her, her damp poncho sprawled over it. "Take the car. The weather's unpredictable, and it's only going to get worse."

Lena looks up. "I'm faster on my bike."

He peers over the frame of his glasses.

"You've seen my times," she adds.

Mr. Peng huffs, conceding without further argument.

Behind her, something heavy thumps on the concrete. Old Man Hsieh reaches for another sandbag and hefts it toward the bay door.

"Ms. Li."

Lena turns back to Mr. Peng, whose eyes flick to his watch. "You should get moving. And remember, I'm leaving early for the biweekly, so send any irregularities well before. I'll be offline." He taps the tablet three times before heading toward his office. "Don't forget. Check the seals."

"Got it."

Mr. Peng is an effective supervisor, firm but not harsh. Lena tries not to dwell on the undertones in his instructions and reminders. Five months as a courier—nearly six now—and she's been late twice, officially warned once. The first delay came only a week into the assignment, after a sleepy truck driver sideswiped her. Her bicycle frame still carries those unrepaired but cosmetic injuries. The second tardiness, however, was entirely her fault. *Her* mind wandered, and she took a wrong turn down the wrong hill.

She crosses to the counter where the day's insulated sleeves are arranged in a neat row. Each one is only a little larger than the palm-sized cartridge it protects, built from a flexible but firm composite with a digital strip showing its matching code and stability readings. The affect drives inside are smooth and rigid and deceivingly hefty considering their thin size.

Lena moves through her list. All drives and their casings report stable humidity and temperature levels, their respective indicators showing the correct blue. On a closer look, one drive is opaque black, an older model, maybe two generations removed. She hasn't seen this version in a while. It has a haze beneath the transparent protective layer, but she eyes the matching blue indices, then double-checks her handheld. It's the one marked for disposal.

"Condensation?"

Lena nearly jumps.

Mr. Peng stands halfway down the shelving row, checking the housing modules.

"Maybe a little," she replies.

He doesn't look surprised. "Replace the sleeve and add an insert just in case. Old stock. I've been telling Management that these seals don't tolerate this humidity."

Lena shows him the matching indicators.

He barely glances over and lifts his chin. "Don't risk it. Anything off, swap it. Your route's manageable enough to spare the extra minute."

So Lena replaces the sleeve, adds a desiccant slip in with the drive, and waits for the fresh case to update its corresponding ID. When it's verified, she adds the red disposal label across its front and back. It'd feel silly, if Lena mulled it over—drives slated for disposal are always rendered inert before transit; there's really no need for all this preventive maintenance. These checks are just procedure, one last formality before destruction, and she has no reason to question why Halcyon does things this way.

When she's done, Lena places the seven sleeves into their individual compartments and presses each cover shut. Seven clean clicks. Seven blue lights along the shell's top display. She scans the case's code into her custody, a chirp and the flash of her handheld confirming the entry. She then slips the package into her insulated and weatherproof Halcyon bag, straps it to the rear rack of her bicycle, and secures everything until the load is balanced. Her handheld disappears into her sling, and with a small wave to Mr. Peng, she tugs on her poncho. Another nod to Old Man Hsieh, who has since arranged the first row of sandbags.

Outside, the rain hangs in a fine sheet. Yellow streetlights gleam against the glossy pavement, and runoff gurgles through the gutters and drains. Somewhere beyond the roofs of neighboring warehouses, a ship horn sounds, bass-heavy and distant. Lena puts on her helmet, flips her hood up, and hops onto the saddle. Her armband trembles once as she clears the property line.

Back on the lower road, she resumes the city's pace. Delivery carts slide past, couriers merge, and cranes shift containers farther down the corridor. Lena keeps to the edge, tracing the bend toward the inner ring of the city's core. At the next crossing, the signal flashes red, and vehicles, cyclists, and scooters congregate while a maintenance truck trundles through. Above them, a billboard pulses: *Better balance starts today*. The lanes clear, and the crowd edges forward again.

The first stop warms up her muscles, sending her into the upper terraces of Meiyu, where the rain recedes. Daybreak filters through the mist to reveal mirrored towers and luxury shops—broad, minimalist spaces with a few careful displays, brands and products her money will never know. For a city obsessed with efficiency, the route makes little sense, uphill and out of the way, but the affluent receive their deliveries first. Lena doesn't mind. The higher districts somehow smell of filtered oxygen and polished wood, and Halcyon's slogans don't crowd the sky here.

She brakes in front of Liang, Sun, & Co. Estate and

Sentiment Management, a holding firm framed by tall glass doors and a manicured garden bordered with sculpted bamboo. Even the pond reflects the motto etched in stone: *Tranquility sustains legacy*. Lena's been here several times, and she still doesn't know what it means.

Inside, the reception space is bathed in tempered light and tastefully perfumed with jasmine. She wedges the case under one arm and removes the single insulated sleeve with the other. A clerk in a pressed navy suit accepts it with a curt nod, then scans her armband. His expression never shifts. Behind him, the translucent partition flashes as her credentials sync—names and timestamps ghost across the surface before fading. She catches only a glimpse, but it's enough to recognize: clients who've authorized emotional inheritance transfers. People who pass along not only property and heirlooms but also raw feelings. Her armband pulses once to confirm the handoff.

"Bequeathal package," the clerk says, tone identical to every other balance-industry professional. He tucks the sleeve into a drawer. "Disposition confirmed."

Though he doesn't look up again, Lena acknowledges him with a tip of her chin as she steps outside.

In the mid-terraces, the other deliveries move quickly. The space between towers narrows, and concrete replaces glass. She makes stops at smaller consulting firms, auxiliary healthcare facilities, and cramped offices. Some drives she drops off at staffed desks; others she places in designated lockers. Each transaction requires a scan, a confirmation, and a pause while the network syncs. Efficiency stretches thin across the day.

Then Lena's handheld pings. A pickup from District 5. The unscheduled disruption is irritating but not unusual. She doesn't question the collection; it happens when another district pushes a system update or another Halcyon courier calls in sick.

When she's completed that errand, the band tightens around her upper arm and *Mandatory Rest Interval* flashes across her handheld. Normally she'd have taken a break, sat down for an actual lunch—the familiar noodle shop or underground food court would pull her in by habit—but the unexpected request has cleaved through her timing and she's not close to either location.

Lena coasts toward a convenience market wedged between two service buildings. The place smells of wet cardboard and tea eggs that have sat in an open pot all day —a little soy sauce, star anise, and the shadow of sulfur. She buys bottled tea and a triangle of pressed rice, eating under the overhang while the counter ticks down. The rest period offers no true relaxation, just another enforced delay. When her armband cinches again, the day has tipped well into the afternoon.

Her stomach a little fuller now, she hops onto her bike and follows the slope into the lower districts where her tires send fans of water outward as she cuts through shallow puddles. When the route marker blinks, Lena realizes it's led her back to the building she passed that morning. The sign for the Halcyon Balance Center looms above the smaller District 3 plaque. It's still strange to her, walking through the main entrance like everyone else; for years she used the staff side door, but five months ago she'd been re-scoped to the customer access.

The clinic is exactly how she left it. The waiting room sits at the front, while two corridors branch behind it: one for Meiyu residents who have Restoration Practitioners clip their emotions for lifestyle and Halcyon benefits, the other for Affect Technicians who process what remains. Lena once worked on the latter side, filtering and diluting the slumps of post-holiday feelings, the sharp aches of love fizzled too fast, the slow corrosion of compounded arguments. She approaches the counter, the insulated sleeve already in hand.

"Lenny! You calibrate your route down to the millisecond again?"

That isn't the usual Halcyon clinic script.

She ignores the lanky man behind the service window and sets her helmet on the counter. He's exaggerating, and wildly. Lena likes her routine and schedules, but not to that extreme.

Soichi leans forward. His thick mop of hair flops into his eyes, and he tugs at his white coat, half-buttoned and smudged at the cuff. His grin is all teeth. "Another batch?" he asks, as if she isn't here almost every week. "No one better to trust with a bag full of feelings." He winks, patting the sill between them. "What've you brought me?"

Lena sets the sleeve down. "Refill. Post-vacation blues, maybe." She doesn't actually know—couriers rarely have that access—but experience from her technician days fills in the guess. "Probably tagged for a new solution."

Barring the different generation models, the drives all look the same on the outside with their clean anonymity, but Lena knows most are consumer-sold stock from the last summer rush, especially if they arrive from the depot —surpluses trimmed and traded in for credits. She used to tone them down and redistribute them as an Affect Technician, the emotional pharmacist of Halcyon's white-coated professions.

Soichi scans her armband, then the sleeve's code, and squints at the terminal. "Yep. For therapeutic blends." He scrolls down the readout. "Return travelers. You sneak a peek?"

The glance he gives her is pure tease; they both know the rules. No one except specifically designated positions with specifically designated clearances can see what's inside the drives. Technicians work with affect tags and ratings, never the raw memories themselves.

"People always sell after vacation," he adds, setting the casing aside. "No one wants the dread of returning to reality. It's always easier to balance before work starts again."

Lena says nothing. She hasn't been on vacation this year, no reason to, not between the former job and reassignment. Demotions usually send people straight to the clinic, but frankly, the change hasn't upset her. The last time she clipped was after the accident. She files the thought away. Just a fact, a record.

"You miss this place?"

She blinks.

"Miss the work? Me?" Soichi leans back and twirls the scanner by its strap around his finger.

"Sure," she replies. She's not sure if she does—she doesn't think about it much—but it seems like the appropriate thing to say.

"Don't know if I ever told you, but I had Zhang Wei give me a little adjustment after you left," he says. "And chased it with my own little cocktail. You know how it goes."

Lena almost smiles at that.

"Wish it'd been yours though. You're still one of the best techs this district's had. Maybe the entire city!"

She grabs her helmet and gives him a shrug. There's nothing useful to say, so she doesn't try.

"It's good to see you, Len. Let me know when we're getting boba or shaved ice. They've opened a new place by the station."

"Sure, Soichi."

He salutes with the scanner as she leaves for her final stop.

It sits near the harbor's edge, a decrepit building marked Waste and Disposal that sees little foot traffic. Industrial-grade materials pass through here, affect drives among them. At the front, the metal door swings open to a poorly lit lobby, and no one greets her. The place doesn't need much staff, maybe a clerk or a maintenance tech on rotation, but in all her runs, she's never encountered either.

Behind a high community table filmed with dust, a row of kiosks idles. The place smells of coolant and stale sea air trapped by concrete. Only one machine functions; the rest wear the same faded signs: OUT OF ORDER or UNDER REPAIR. They've been that way since Lena started.

She scans her armband, and the screen flickers then freezes. On the second attempt, it wakes and flips to the next display of instructions. Lena produces the last drive, wipes its casing on her shirt, and scans.

ERROR: UNVERIFIED CLIENT

She checks the strip and code with her handheld. Everything matches. She tries again, but the machine spits out the same rejection. Switching to manual input, Lena fights the sluggish touchscreen, the cursor drifting too far right with each press. After multiple attempts, the slot below unlocks with a reluctant click. The terminal accepts the sleeve, then opens its jaws halfway through the verification sequence. The display pops up:

HUMIDITY ALERT

Then—

TRANSFER LOCKED

Crouching, Lena studies the drive. Though the cover's indicator glows blue, the cartridge's status light now vacillates between blue and green. Inside the casing, the desiccant still looks dry. She opens the sleeve carefully, touching both unit and insert, and confirms they *are* dry. She closes it and tries the machine's process once more. This time, the kiosk whirs back to life, stutters, ejects the piece again, and falls silent mid-cycle.

Her attention darts toward the office window, shutters drawn and dark. Of course. Predictable, but frustrating all the same.

And for the first time all day, her pulse quickens—not from physical exertion or fear, but from a hairline fracture in the stillness she keeps, pressure edging in on a shift that should've wrapped up cleanly. The unanticipated pickup, the detour to her routine, the incomplete delivery —it all accumulates.

Annoyed, Lena checks the time. The depot is closing soon and she's not letting this inconvenience end the day. She re-cases the drive and heads for the exit.

TWO

Outside the disposal site, the rain has committed. Lena's armband pings and she knows her handheld is prompting her to confirm the completion of her route. She ignores it. If she pushes hard, she might still make it to the depot before Mr. Peng locks up.

She fastens the strap across her bag and starts pedaling toward the city's heart. The disposal site sits in the lower districts on the other side of a hill, but cutting through shaves time, even with the ascent. The incline gnaws at her legs, and her lungs are working hard by the midpoint. Her armband pulses twice, informing of exertion and elevated biometrics—a reminder she disparages, as if she doesn't know it already.

At the top, red and white barriers descend across the road. A drone hovers above, bouncing with the weather, its amplified voice flat: "Transit hold. Causeway closure in effect. Please remain in place."

The surrounding traffic halts in orderly rows, and Lena checks the time again. Minutes are counting down to an incomplete route and her second official warning.

As she waits, she opens a channel and types:

> Disposal delivery incomplete. Verification and machine failure. Bringing back for review.

The message sends while rain taps her poncho in dull bursts. Droplets gather on her screen, magnifying and distorting the empty field where a reply should be. She wipes it clear and waits. One minute. Two. Mr. Peng is normally responsive, but still nothing.

When the barriers retract, Lena rides for the depot anyway. At this point, she knows it's futile, but the motion is necessary. This has been a deviation from schedule, from expected order, and she's trying to remedy it however she can. Frustration builds as she approaches the closed gates. Beyond them, the bay door is down, sandbags neatly stacked along its lip.

Lena grips her handlebars. All she needed was to return the drive. She'd been so close. In the bag behind her, the case is near empty, just the one defective nuisance within it. It's one thing to be late or to have an incomplete delivery—both draw official warnings. Collect enough of those, it becomes a compliance demerit. But keeping Halcyon drives past business hours? Unauthorized possession is an immediate strike. Three strikes and she'd be reassigned again, *demoted* again to the next undesirable job. But what choice does she have? Mr. Peng isn't responding, the depot's closed, and the report is already deficient.

Reluctantly, Lena turns and merges into the evening flow, heading toward the residential blocks. Rain lacquers the streets, headlights cut pale ribbons through it, and the gravity of the looming consequences presses against her. It's another narrowing of tolerance she doesn't know if she can take much more of.

She knows she shouldn't have brought the drive home, but for all her tardiness—two to be exact; one not her fault—she's never *not* completed her route. If not for the delays, if not for the pickup that threw her schedule, if not for the glitched-out kiosk, it would've just been another delay. She would've gotten back to the depot, Mr. Peng would have reviewed the error, retagged the drive, and either redirected her to another disposal site or assigned another courier, like when she'd filled in for District 5. Or held it for the next day, the next schedule. But now she's sitting on a violation because she's never been in this situation, never been told what to do, and her supervisor *still* hasn't replied.

By the time she arrives at her building and hangs her poncho over her locked bicycle frame, she's already convinced herself that the fix is simple. She'll open the sleeve, check the fault, retag the drive, and deliver it first thing tomorrow well before her shift. Lena's done similar troubleshooting as a Halcyon technician. And though her logs will show a different date and time at completion, it'll still *be* a completion. That should lessen the blow. It's a way forward, a solution.

She climbs the stairs and ducks past the second floor.

The main door is propped open, the exterior mesh screen giving her neighbor a full view of anyone coming or going. She takes the next flight two steps at a time and quickly enters her flat on the third. It's spacious, too much for one, but it's hers and quiet.

Lena hangs her helmet and sets the courier bag on the half-living room, half-kitchen table. Ignoring the pinch of hunger, she steps into the short hall, past a closed pink door, and fetches the calibration kit from her bedroom. It has been sitting on the shelf above her desk under a stack of training manuals she hasn't touched in years.

The machine is outdated, long replaced in most clinics and offices, the seals brittle and the old Halcyon logo faded. And though it was meant to be a training device, the tools still function: a compact scanner, an attachable secondary port for merging and diluting affects, a set of alignment probes for confining and adjusting tags, and its cable-based apparatus. Lena blows the dust off the display's cover and stops. She enjoyed her time, for the most part, as an Affect Technician. It's a memory that comes and goes.

She received the kit early on, when they'd wanted the techs to practice, to keep up with the advancing technology. She should've returned the equipment after leaving the clinic, but no one ever asked for it, and Lena never volunteered. In truth, she'd forgotten about its existence until her ride back. Of course, it's another tally to the reasons why she should just accept the coming punishment, why she shouldn't mess with the defective drive. But she's still annoyed that none of this is her fault and she's here now. It's an easy adjustment, she tells herself.

Lena lugs the unit to the table, plugs it in, and powers on the chamber. Its internal fan spins to life, and the machine's indicator glows its familiar blue. Clearing a space to the side, she carefully removes the drive from its sleeve.

"Just evaluate the error and retag it," she murmurs. "That's all."

Easy. She scans the cartridge, locks it in the docking compartment, and closes the glass lid. The kit purrs as the program starts, but then the light on both drive and machine pulses synchronously. Once. Twice. The vibration deepens into a tone she doesn't recognize, and the chamber's indicator shifts to a color that shouldn't exist, a shade between green and yellow.

Lena frowns as she connects the calibration line from the terminal to her armband, which squeezes once at the confirmed link. It's a relief, considering the technological generation gap. She follows the screen as it feeds a stream of data: stability curves, humidity trace, affect frequency variance. Nothing unusual in the internal metrics. Except the light's color.

She taps the panel into the next setting. A deeper dive. The fan speed increases, a slight alteration in its sound like the entire note has been transposed a half-step higher. And she waits. A shimmer moves across the transparent lid, shadows shifting within the glass like a gleam beneath water. The readout on the side display glitches, and something in the calibration link misfires, resulting in another squeeze to her arm.

Before she can check, sound bleeds. A distant thrum that isn't the chamber's, something like a muffled crowd, somewhere open but not. Then somehow, the scent of oil, crisp dough, and the smoke of a griddle. Impossible, but distinct. Taste follows, salt at the edge of her tongue. It's a strange feeling—hearing, smelling, tasting all this knowing it's not happening. She's sitting in her quarters where she can still smell the air that's sat a bit too long, a mix of soap within it. These other sensations aren't real. And most of all, this is wrong. Her apparatus only reads tagged affect signatures, not this. Not sensory detail.

The images disappear like wisps of smoke, and Lena's spine snaps straight. She sits several seconds, staring blankly. She knows what this is. A clip. But not inert. Drives bound for disposal are neutralized before transit. This one shouldn't contain anything. She should shut it down. Eject it, seal it, and report the fault.

Instead, she reaches for the probe set, adjusts the cable's connection, then activates the application once more. This time, the shimmer comes again, sharpening into unknown outlines. Shades bleed like watercolor, faint but present, and then warmth flushes in Lena's core.

Oil and metal meet with a hiss. Nearby, a knife works through fresh green scallions. Scent unfurls as dough slaps a hot surface and begins to firm, starch turning elastic, glossing before it crisps. An egg cracks, yolk bright like a sun held in a single drop, then fingers fold the pancake, press the seams, and coax the steam outward in a rush that carries onion, oil, and cooked dough together into a single, full breath. Raindrops tap out a syncopated percussion against the stall. Metal ladles rattle nearby, and vendors call to each other over the crowd's murmur. A stool scrapes, someone laughs, conversation holds. The air stirs, carrying everything with it, the scent, the heat, the smoke, turning the narrow lane into a corridor of flavor. A plain paper sleeve crinkles and imprints a flush of heat across her palm. The *cōng yóu bǐng*,[1] the scallion pancake, flakes under her bite, a crackle giving way to layers that yield green onion, egg, and salty dough. A streak of chili crisp blooms across her tongue, heat accompanying the freshness of basil nestled inside.

It all sweeps through Lena with startling speed. And behind it, a sensation arrives fast, immense and uncontained. Her chest tightens, not with pain but pressure, as if the feeling has nowhere to go. Her breath stutters, her vision blurs, and her body struggles to hold something it's not used to.

Lena jerks back, the cable disconnecting with a pop. The glow in the chamber drains to blue and holds. The flat is still, but everything within her is in free fall. She ignores the pulsing band against her muscles, her heart pounding more than it had on the hill ascent, more than it probably has since the accident.

Because she knows what this feeling is.

Joy.

THREE

Morning filters through the kitchen window and strikes the counter. For a moment, the residence is suspended in glass. In the adjoining space, the drive rests where Lena left it on the table.

By reflex, she reaches for a mug above the sink before remembering she's already made tea. Her white-glazed ceramic mug waits near the drying rack, its steam feathering upward. She holds the drink to her lips and draws in the black tea's scent—malty with a trace of honey beneath. She stares at her handheld and its last message received.

Bring to the depot immediately. Holding overnight violates procedure.

No greeting. No sign-off. Exact, as expected. She can picture Mr. Peng typing it, brows slanting down behind his glasses, that crease of disapproval he saves for late reports and misplaced sleeves.

She sets the cup down and exhales through her nose. The malfunctioning kiosk, the causeway stoppage, and the closed depot weren't Lena's fault. She replays the sequence as if it might lessen the pressure, although she knows Halcyon logs results, not circumstances.

However, she *does* own some fault. The drive looks ordinary, sitting there on the table, no different from any she's previously carried and delivered, yet the echo of this one's sensations and emotion cling to the space the way a smell lingers in fabric. She takes a deep breath and swears she can still catch a hint of oil and dough. It isn't vivid anymore, but it's enough to disrupt the quiet she's built around herself.

Her focus shifts to the other drive on the opposite side of the calibration kit: a blank service unit she wiped in the middle of the night when sleep wouldn't come. A mirrored copy would take less than a minute. Lena could call it precaution or even procedure, archiving a faulty drive. Or possibly stretch her reasoning and say she's protecting company property and interests.

But the real truth is she can't bear the idea of losing the joy she felt. All of this is unfamiliar ground, and her hesitation is no different. Lena follows rules and regulations, not one to debate herself, and still she's unsure how she's gotten here. She's spent years letting procedure or someone else decide for her. Questioning never helped, so she's learned not to do it. Yet something in her hand twitches, perhaps a tremor leftover from the previous night or something new. A quiet disobedience.

By the time she acknowledges the choice, her fingers are already moving. She connects the cable to her armband, slots the drive into the chamber, places the empty one into the secondary port, and waits as the menu blinks awake. The kit's outdated and unpatched, but it still carries a dormant option at the very bottom.

MIRROR BACKUP

Raw-sector duplication. A maintenance tool only.

Drives shed fidelity with every transfer, more so for older models. It won't be a one-for-one copy, especially with a drive that's meant to hold training sequences, not actual affects. Static will creep into the channels, edges will fray, and details will be lost. A proper recovery unit and terminal would preserve more, but Lena doesn't have that convenience or access.

She wavers. What is she thinking?

Halcyon says their audits catch everything, but Lena knows from experience that nothing short of a crisis ever draws their attention; this little transgression likely won't register at all. She assures herself, then authorizes the command.

On the display, the progress bar creeps across, a slender white line against black. She ignores the blinking option underneath to cancel this misconduct, and when the process completes its run, a tone rings out, barely a note.

Lena sits and stares. That's two drives now. Two versions of a feeling she is not willing to surrender.

When her alarm goes off, reminding her of a judgment yet to come, she reverently slips the original back into its sleeve, sets it in its case, then into her courier bag. She returns the calibration kit to the shelf above her desk and before she can reconsider, she stows the duplicate in a closet drawer beneath a folded pajama set she hasn't worn in a long time. As if concealment were a skill she'd only recently learned.

Meanwhile, her tea cools on the counter, forgotten.

Lena locks the door behind her, helmet cradled under one arm. Outside her flat, the building feels off. Not bad, not good, but different. The hallway smells of watered soil and her neighbor's morning ritual, a warning that Mrs. Kuan's door downstairs is propped open.

Just before the second-floor landing, the air shifts. Oil catches and sings, and Lena freezes, one foot poised above the next step, pinned by the sound. For an instant, she's back in the drive's memory with the sizzle of heat, the scent of scallion and dough.

But it isn't the same.

Egg, yes. Scallion, yes. But there's a toasty sweetness that doesn't match. This different sensation rises, tugging beneath her ribs.

"Morning, dear," Mrs. Kuan calls out.

Lena doesn't know how the old woman can tell it's her; she's not heavy with her feet.

"You're early. Heading off to work?"

Caught now, betrayed by the smell, Lena answers, "Yes, auntie." Thankfully, it's her last shift before a day off. She quickly remembers her manners, adds a "good morning," then pauses just outside the screen door, listening to the susurration from the pan inside.

"Work, work." Mrs. Kuan chortles. She turns from her stove, sleeves rolled to the elbow, a red apron tied around her waist. Her hair is permed, black with white roots showing through, just enough to signal she's due for another dye soon. Under the kitchen light, the shade is slightly off, the kind of color that never quite matches the model on the box.

"You look pale. *Chiah pá bōe?*[*] Here. I've made *dàn bǐng*.[1] Eat one before you go."

Egg crêpes. Not the crisp scallion pancakes from the affect drive.

"Oh, no, I'm fine," Lena says automatically, hand rising in polite refusal. Even as her gut gurgles.

"Nonsense. You haven't eaten yet; I can hear it in your voice. You can't be *fine* on an empty stomach."

"Oh, it's too much trouble," Lena insists, though without conviction. "I really shouldn't."

"Silly girl." Mrs. Kuan waves her excuses away and turns back to the pan. Her spatula scrapes against metal as she folds the crêpe over itself until it's a narrow strip. She slides it onto a napkin and sprinkles some dark sauce over it.

Lena pulls the screen door open to help, and Mrs. Kuan holds it wide with a slippered foot. She catches Lena's empty hand with firm resolve and presses the dàn

---

[*] Have you eaten?

bǐng into it. "Here. *Chiah-pñg!** Before it gets cold. I made too many and they won't taste right reheated."

The warmth sinks into Lena's palm at once, the dàn bǐng soft and pliant, giving slightly when she adjusts her grip. Lena *is* hungry, though in this context, etiquette has taught her to pretend otherwise. Under Mrs. Kuan's stare, she takes a bite. The crêpe is tender, the texture relenting between her teeth. Dark golden spots mottle the surface, and the taste comes together savory between the egg and scallion with a subtle sweetness from the wrapper and thick soy sauce. It finds her belly, nestling deeper than she expects, and an ache follows, flickers, then fades.

"Why don't you come in and sit?"

Lena covers her mouth and shakes her head. "I have to go."

"You've been busy," Mrs. Kuan says, wiping her hands on her apron.

Lena nods, finishing another bite.

"Hm." The old woman's gaze lifts to the stairwell. "The building's been too quiet these days, and I don't care for it."

Lena doesn't answer.

"Ah, you remind me of my son when he's working too much." Mrs. Kuan holds out the screen door until Lena takes it, then moves back to the stove where batter and ingredients wait.

Lena wonders who the extra food is for. In all the years she's lived here, she's never seen anyone else coming and going into the flat.

----

* Eat!

"Always running off," Mrs. Kuan continues. "Never sitting down long enough to finish a meal."

"I eat," Lena says, swallowing the last of the crêpe.

"You nibble." The woman's voice softens. "Eat properly once in a while. You'll get some color back and put some meat on those bones."

Lena wipes her fingers with the napkin, then folds and slips it into her pocket. "I'll try."

"That's all I ask." Another stream of batter hits the pan. "And tell the university not to grind you down. The city forgets we're human."

"Yes, auntie."

"Good girl." Mrs. Kuan waves her off. "Now go, or you'll be late. Take care, Mara."

Lena doesn't bother to correct Mrs. Kuan. Her neighbor has never gotten her name right, but that's Lena's fault. She's never stopped long enough for a real conversation. As she heads down, the heat of the dàn bǐng lingers on her hand and the flavor of egg and scallion clings to her tongue. Behind her, Mrs. Kuan's soft warble of a song carries through the stairwell.

By the time Lena rolls up to the depot, the rain has tapered into a consistent gray wash like the previous day. She threads through the gap left in the line of sandbags guarding the edge and ducks beneath the partially raised bay door. Old Man Hsieh sits at his post with his dented thermos and the same half-awake expression. When she passes, he gives a brief nod, and she returns it with a smile that is more grimace. It's clear she's about to face discipline, perhaps an added sharp word or two.

And at the intake counter, Mr. Peng is waiting. His tablet is laid neatly in front of him, stylus tapping against its frame as if he's been standing there for some time. As she scans in, Lena glances at one of the digital clocks. She's actually early.

"You held the unit overnight," Mr. Peng starts, nudging his spectacles higher on the bridge of his nose.

Not his usual greeting.

Lena braces herself and unfastens the courier bag. "Yes, sir. I sent the message yesterday."

"I saw." The stylus stills. "That isn't procedure."

"I tried to make it back. The depot was already closed, and I couldn't leave it outside so I brought it home. It was kept safe, I promise." She considers adding more, that it never left the Halcyon case, but that's a lie.

"The drive?"

Lena extracts the sleeve, moves closer, and sets it on the counter. The casing is clean, the red disposal label bright on both sides. Mr. Peng pulls the drive out and scans it. If he notices anything, he gives no sign. His features hardly move.

Lena swallows, an internal sound crackling in her ears. She's relieved she hadn't adjusted the disposal-site code. She hadn't altered anything else either, at least nothing that would give her away. And so far, the impact of a compliance strike hasn't landed and its threat seems to ease.

"The disposal machine wouldn't take it," she says. "I tried. Multiple times."

"Did you do the manual input? The kiosks are finicky in conditions like this."

"Yes. It accepted my entry then shut down halfway through."

Mr. Peng notes something on his tablet, then takes the drive to the machine at the end of the first row—a waist-high console enclosed in clear composite, its surface set with a recessed slot, interface, and a single light bar. The neutralizer grumbles as he powers it on and slides the cartridge in.

"Today's schedule and deliveries are ready," he says, not looking back. "Go ahead, get started."

With that, Lena begins running through the laid-out set of sleeves, though her attention keeps tracking toward Mr. Peng.

After a few moments, he clears his throat.

"Everything fine, sir?" she asks.

He makes another ambiguous sound.

When the neutralizer idles, Lena's nearly finished her checks. Mr. Peng returns to the counter, where he reseals the drive in a fresh sleeve and applies a new red disposal label. He holds it out.

"Am I in trouble?" she asks, taking it.

He pauses fractionally longer than usual. Then, almost absentmindedly, he adjusts his glasses, clears his throat, and picks up his stylus. "No." Mr. Peng marks something on his tablet. "I'll log the variance and resolve this. It'll return to your queue."

Relief comes in a heavy wave. She's not sure what's

just happened. She's somehow avoided a penalty that wasn't hers to bear, at least not for the malfunctioning kiosk and incomplete delivery.

"Oh, Mr. Peng. Perhaps a different disposal site this time? The machines—"

"Yes, yes."

Lena doesn't realize the adjusted route stretches farther across the city until she's left the depot.

By midday, her shift has held without incident or interruption. No broken terminals, no surprise pickups, and no unexpected detours. She's ahead of schedule, every checkpoint cleared clean. It should be satisfying, being efficient and on time, but the order of it all feels insubstantial. The old drive marked for disposal is gone, off her queue, and Lena feels a twinge of disappointment at its quick and seamless disappearance—no errors or issues this time. She forces herself not to think about the duplicate in her closet and focuses on the road.

It dips toward the lower quarter, where rain has pooled and refuses to move on. The drains here can't keep pace this week, and the air is tinged with minerals leached from old pipes and the sourness of standing water. Lena coasts to a stop beneath a patched awning, shakes off her poncho, and props her bicycle against the wall, its kickstand catching on a groove on a flaked brick.

The sign above the narrow frontage buzzes, one light out so it reads XIAO NO DLE HOUSE. As she steps inside, the entry chime gives a single bright note. It's her usual stop when she can spare time for an actual lunch, far enough from the depot that Halcyon's demands blur but close enough to return without cutting it too close. And the small restaurant fits her appetite and schedule. Simple, the way she prefers her breaks.

In the tight space, heat gathers, easing the moisture from her sleeve, while the honey-colored interior lends a gentle warmth. The shop is subdued, just early enough that the lunch crowd hasn't arrived yet. Behind the L-shaped counter, a woman about Lena's age works between two large industrial pots. Brown highlights intertwine with the darker lengths of her hair, twisting in a loose spiral of a bun. Her bangs fall forward, shadowing her eyes.

"Hi! Let me guess," Runi says with a smile. "Top shelf again?" The owner-cook is already stretching for the packets stacked above. "Or do we risk real broth today?"

Lena raises her palm, and Runi laughs.

"It's consistent," Lena says, taking her place on the worn stool at the furthest end.

"Consistent," Runi echoes with a groan. "I spend hours kneading and shaping noodles with the perfect chew, hours building broth that could wake the dead, and you"—she pinches and tears the packet open, tossing aside toppings and seasoning sachets—"want the powdered version."

"It's predictable."

"Yes. Predictably tragic."

Still, Runi drops the puck of dried noodles inside the same chipped blue bowl Lena has used since her first month as a courier. She pours boiling water, leaning on the counter as steam rises between them. While Lena opens the chopstick box, Runi shakes in the seasoning and toppings, the liquid turning a familiar amber as they dissolve. The smell—mild spice, far too much sodium—hooks something behind Lena's breastbone.

Runi hovers an overturned plate above the bowl and arches an eyebrow. "How about a curl of ginger this time? A few onions? Maybe a bit of beef tendon to mix it up?"

Lena only lifts her hand again.

"One day..." Runi says, lifting the bowl over the median and placing it in front of Lena with care. "I'll get you to order something that actually requires effort."

Lena flashes a cordial smirk. Technically, these noodles demand effort as well.

As she waits for the strands to soften, the radio switches to a slow ballad in the background. Warm vapor swirls the window, softening the street beyond, and under her breath, Runi follows the jazzy melody, the tune carried by the percussion of her ladle and the murmuring from the pots behind her.

When the dish is ready, Lena eats. Normally she finishes quickly and slips back into her route, but today the shop's ambience settles around her. The powdered broth is weak beside the richer scents in the shop—garlic and ginger, beef bones in a long simmer with soy sauce, onions, a trace of chili oil, and fresh greens. Lena takes another mouthful, thoughts sliding to the morning and the absence of disciplinary action. Not even a strike or a warning. She considers Mr. Peng's reaction, his subtle dismissal, and correction. But then the memory from last night brushes close again. The aftertaste of scallion, oil, and dough, and of the unbridled joy that had moved through her.

The shop chime sounds, jolting Lena's attention back to her surroundings. Runi smiles as another customer steps in, then drifts toward the stove, lifting a lid to release a veil of steam.

Lena lowers her chopsticks, the spell gone. She slurps up the rest of her meal in a few quick pulls, sets the bowl aside, and wipes her mouth and hands. By the time she touches her armband to the scanner beside the register, the lunch rush begins.

"Next time, real broth!" Runi calls out just as the door closes behind Lena, cutting off the growing chatter, the music, and the scent of slow-cooked beef.

For a moment, Lena stands under the awning and the leftover warmth clings longer than usual, before the ongoing rain cools it away.

Night drapes itself over the island. Through Lena's window, towers shine white and amber against massed clouds bruised by the incoming storm. The muted thrum from the main road continues, steady as breath.

The day has unfolded as the system intends: route covered, deliveries confirmed, each checkpoint cleared without error. But still, the pattern feels wrong. Since lunch—possibly before—something has shadowed every stop and verification signature. Lena is no stranger to wandering distractions, but today her mind slips more than usual, and now at home, the sensations return like fragmented specters. Heat on metal. Nearby laughter. The sudden flare of jubilation.

That isn't hers. It *doesn't* belong to her.

On her desk, the copied drive rests in her calibration kit's chamber, and the menu and its populated command field spreads open. This old test unit can't hold the same nuance as the original; it lacks the neural fidelity of newer models—of even the outdated original's iteration—and can't carry the same texture or depth. She's never experienced it—no one is allowed to, of course—but she knows that affects degrade in transfer, leaving images and tags, but stripped of raw sensation. There's little point in having mirrored the drive. The original that holds the full feeling has been wiped and destroyed, and this version is a mere fraction of what it was.

In front of her, the delete prompt waits. One touch would erase the file and restore order to her and Halcyon's values.

Balance earns trust. Balance earns stability.

Lena was never meant to witness those inputs, never meant to feel what somebody else chose to clip and discard. The cartridge only sits here now because the original was supposed to be inert. And it's a reduced version. Yet her hand does not move to erase it.

Instead, she dismisses the interface with a sharp motion. Her fingers hover over the apparatus cable, and a prickle of wrongness climbs up her spine, a boundary she feels rather than names. For a second, she almost retreats from it, but the hesitation fails. She connects the line.

The response that follows is different. Static washes across the small display and resolves into motion on the chamber lid. Shapes form as the memory plays, dulled and incomplete. Lanterns flutter above narrow stalls, oil ripples across a griddle. A hand flips a pancake, presses it flat, and breaks an egg over the center. A puff of vapor rises, but no scent follows. There's no sound either, only color and movement.

The image then stutters. It's unfinished, yet the memory and emotion beckons all the same. Just seeing these fragments, Lena basks in the residue of bliss.

"Who would give this up?" she whispers.

And the question hangs.

In the kit's dormant screen, her reflection wavers. A woman looks back at her. For a heartbeat, Lena thinks it's someone else, but recognition settles and she lets out a breath. Whoever severed this feeling did so with purpose. And for the first time in a very long while, Lena begins to question. She wants to know why.

FOUR

Sleep keeps its distance, but when Lena finally sinks under, the memory sits close, caressing her even in the veil of partial dreams. She wakes just before dawn with the impression of it still pressed against her cheek. Steam. The hiss of a hot plate. Someone laughing beside her. It falls apart the moment she tries to hold it.

Lena pushes upright and crosses the room, drawn toward the desk by the calm blue inside the contraption. The color emits and scatters under the housing, softer than yesterday. She switches the kit on, resting her hand over the lid as it warms up. She doesn't bother with the cable or armband; this version doesn't have that connectivity anyway. With a shallow exhale, she triggers the playback.

The images come again. Not as vivid, not as complete. But they arrive, and with them, Lena remembers the burst of elation. It still hitches her breath. Leaning closer as the sequence runs out, she chases the last ghost of heat, willing it to stay in her skin, as if proximity can coax the original clarity back. But it slides away. The dip hits the base of her sternum, and her body reacts—breath snagged and shoulders tight, as though straining for something just out of reach. It all ends too quickly, leaving a space that spreads beneath her ribs, a need she has no language for, only the sense of being cut off mid-conversation.

Whatever remains inside this duplicate is already fraying. Even without checking its stability readings, without replaying it, Lena knows the copied segment is deteriorating on its own. She's already been stripped of its sensations, its sound, smell, taste, and texture. And on top of that, she hasn't been able to pull any identifying characteristics or clues as to where or who or when this memory is from. The idea of losing that brightness, even its broken version, stings.

Barely noticing the wrinkles in her clothes or the growing mess in her room, Lena dresses quickly. She's taken this setup as far as it will go; the unit's time and fidelity is decaying. She's combed through the mirrored data logs, but there's only so much she can do. Her home equipment won't give her anything new.

But perhaps...

"Soichi will know," she says.

She pauses, but her voice has no company in the empty flat. And since it's her day off, and no one has argued her statement, that's that.

Lena seats the drive into a piece of plain paper and folds it until it's completely covered. Her handheld blinks with a Halcyon account notice, but she dismisses it with a swipe and slots the device and wrapped cartridge into her sling. Then she leaves, careful to give a quick wave through Mrs. Kuan's screen before her neighbor can call out. It's Lena's day off, but she isn't giving it over to rest.

The morning light has the tint of unpolished steel, and she rides toward the clinic, following a path that needs no deliberation. When she arrives, a handful of people sit spaced along the waiting benches, their faces dulled. The room carries a brooding quiet, thickened by rain-soaked coats and the unspoken weight everyone has brought in with them. Lena recognizes the signs—seasonal malaise or what the practitioners call weather blues. The storms always push a few more through the doors. When she approaches the service window, the drive's added bulk against her chest seems to have gained a few kilograms.

It isn't Soichi today.

A younger technician Lena doesn't recognize glances up with practiced courtesy. "Hello. How can we help you this beautiful morning?"

"Is Soichi in?"

The tech hesitates. "Do you have an appointment or are you a walk-in? I can take your order or prescription—"

"Oh no, I'm just—"

Before Lena can finish, a voice carries down the hall behind the partition. "Is that who I think it is?"

Her former colleague leans out from an internal doorway, a sleek visor and headset perched over his thick hair. His expression brightens when he spots her. "I knew it! Charlotte, let Lenny through, please."

"What? We're not supposed to—"

"Oh, don't be a spoilsport."

The technician shoots him a mild glare but doesn't argue further. The inner door clicks open, and for a brief second, Lena considers telling Charlotte that it's okay, she used to work there, to rationalize, but she doesn't. Soichi waves Lena in with his usual unhurried ease and as she joins him, it's like slipping back into an old uniform. His workspace resembles the others—a small office with a narrow table, twin monitors, and a jumble of diagnostic cables and prods beside an interface rig. He drags a spare chair from the adjoining office.

"Hey, that's mine!" Charlotte hisses, head poking around the corner.

"You have two!" Soichi answers. "Share your blessings."

Lena swears she hears the technician at the front desk grumble, and she gives Soichi a look.

He rolls his eyes. "She loves me, don't worry." He squeezes the chair beside his setup and gestures for Lena to sit. "But you. I was about to file a complaint for neglect."

"I saw you two days ago."

"Neglect," he insists. "What have you brought me? Breakfast?"

"No," she says, sitting. "Sorry. And no deliveries."

He grunts. "You're no fun at all, but fine. I accept your presence as currency. For now." Soichi slides a tray of affect drives onto a minicart and wheels it aside. "So what brings you to my fine temple of adjustment?"

Lena glances toward the open hallway and nudges the door closed with the tip of her shoe. She fidgets with her crossbody sling, worrying the edges of the cartridge's imprint. "I...need a deep dive...to check a code."

Soichi's eyebrows rocket up.

Lena swallows, hoping it isn't too noticeable.

"Oho." He folds his arms. "No breakfast, no deliveries, and now a rogue courier checking code? Back to crime, I see."

She huffs, nearly protesting, then decides it's only Soichi joking again. "If anything, it's back to *work*," Lena corrects. "On my day off."

"Yes." His teeth flash. "The *worst* kind of crime." He points toward the diagnostics bench. "So, what are we working with?"

Lena exhales and slides the sleeve from her chest pack. She places it on the table. "Can you access the originator data from this?"

Soichi's brows lift again, but if he has another question or opinion, he keeps it to himself. He turns the copy over in his hand, inspecting the training unit casing, then holds her in a long assessment.

Lena only shrugs.

He mirrors the gesture, then inserts the drive into the console port. The interface hums and Lena leans in, close enough to follow the scrolling text without crowding his elbow. Already the system is recovering more than her old kit ever could.

Soichi squints, drops his visor properly over his eyes, then whistles low. "Could you have dug up an older model than this?"

Lena's certain he doesn't expect an actual answer to

that question. "Can you pull the originator?" she asks instead.

"Code like this hasn't been around in ages."

"It was a regular drive," she replies—meaning the original unit. "An older generation."

"Sure, that makes sense in casing, maybe. What generation though? Maybe it was transferred under new protocols..." he says, partially to himself, "but this affect signature is ancient. Halcyon dropped this kind of splice format before their major overhaul." He turns to her. "Where did you get this, Lena?"

She weighs whether to shape a lie, but the delay would give it away. She braces instead. "The original—" Not the original, apparently, if Soichi is correct. Lena shakes her head. "The drive was flagged for disposal. The machine threw errors—humidity and some other stuff. I couldn't bring it back on time to the—" She pauses and takes a breath. "Here's the thing. The whole situation went sideways and I ended up taking it home. I figured I could fix the issue myself and return it."

Soichi thumbs his headset upward and looks askance at her. "Did you...open this 'original'?" He curls his fingers in the air.

Her silence answers for her.

"And you copied it," he says, slower and quieter now.

Lena doesn't hear a question, so she doesn't confirm or deny, but the evidence is there in front of them.

Soichi leans back and grimaces, rubbing his neck. "I'm guessing you already tried to find the data and couldn't, which is why you're here. Why *this* is here."

She inclines her head.

"And here I assumed you missed me." Before Lena can stumble over more nonanswers, Soichi graciously continues. "Well, you didn't find anything because this isn't complete."

Lena's frown deepens. She'd considered the possibility that the copy hadn't mirrored everything. She'd assumed it was her outdated kit or that she'd overlooked something else.

"This isn't whole. You remember this coding predates full single-stream mapping, right?"

She only looks back at him. Somewhere, a distant synapse fires—a scrap of orientation footage, a slide she never lingered on, knowledge learned once and set aside.

"This is way back when Halcyon used to clip in pairs. Weren't you paying attention?" Soichi makes a face. "Huh. It has been years...but there was a refresher training module, remember? The old-school process used twin drives for balance and integration." He jerks his chin toward the console. "Hang on, maybe I can trace the partner link..." The rest he mutters to himself, fingers already moving over the keyboard attachment, translating intent to action.

Lena bends closer as credentials and archive indices scroll, stall, and blink—waiting for the intersection of lives to surface. The pull resolves to a single result. One line. A dead link.

"Typical," Soichi mumbles. "Corrupted. Probably in the transfer." His eyes flick to her. "And the subsequent duplication."

"Can you restore it?"

"Am I a miracle worker?" He grins, working the

machine a bit more, then jabs a button with a satisfying mechanical clack. He sits back as the display cursor spins, then stops.

But nothing new appears.

It's still the one line. Still dead.

Lena tries and fails to school her disappointment.

Soichi's smile also droops. "Not these kinds of miracles, I guess." He taps the console with a knuckle. "But I can dig a bit more. Maybe file an inquiry on the counterpart if you want. The link's broken but a manual search and requisition *could* drag something up."

"You'd do that?"

He shrugs. "It's a long shot, and it'll take a day or more if it's even on record, but if it's already been processed or disposed of, there's not much either of us can do."

He studies her again, and Lena notes a small stain on the carpet. Coffee, or knowing Soichi, some milk-tea concoction.

"Len, what does this mean to you, anyway? Is it yours —" He stops himself. "No, it can't be. Unless you clipped this when you were a baby... And Halcyon doesn't allow that. Not yet, at least."

Lena lifts her gaze to the console and the drive inside. "It was marked for disposal. I just—I didn't want to lose the data integrity."

"Right." He ejects the cartridge and slides it across.

She places her hand on the copy but doesn't take it. She imagines him seeing it, feeling it, even in this faded and limited state. Maybe he could help her track its source, its owner. She coaxes it back and glances at his terminal. "Do you..."

Soichi's hands fly up. "Whoa. That's a big no-no, Lenny. Don't drag me into your bad—well, *more* into your bad decisions."

Her shoulders slump.

"What exactly...did you see?" he asks after a moment, voice subdued.

Lena traces the drive with a fingertip. "It wasn't just seeing, it was—" She exhales at length, searching for the right explanation. "It was in my body. I could hear it...I could *feel* it."

"What?"

She tries again. "It started with smell, I think. Fried dough and green onions. Then the sound...that egg cracking. And laughing. I didn't see them, didn't see anyone, but I just knew they were there."

He waits, eyes wide and lips parted.

"And the...happiness," she says at last. The word lands clumsily. She shrinks in on herself, heat flushing up her neck. "It was so strong. It just came with everything else. All at once. There was so much of it."

Soichi squints. "You felt *happiness*?"

"Yes."

There's no doubt.

"Huh" is all he says. He leans back. "That's an odd emotion to clip..." He ponders for a moment, straightens, and then claps his hands once. "All right, so this is about food, then?"

Lena straightens. "Yes. Cōng yóu bǐng."

"Oh. Delicious," Soichi says. "This is promising."

"Promising?"

"Was it a home? Restaurant? Food court? Commercial kitchen?"

"No, I think a—a stall."

"Like at a night market?" He brightens. "That's something."

She nods.

He smacks the table with the palm of his hand. "You could go the human route!"

"What?"

"You know, old-fashioned detective work! Visit the markets. Ask around. Talk to people. Describe what you can and see if anyone recognizes it."

Lena flinches inward. He makes it sound so easy. That means conversation. With *people*. With strangers. Soichi is an exception, a tolerated colleague. But others? That's different. Lena isn't the extroverted one; she has no interest in turning herself into someone who approaches people. Her chest starts to constrict.

He laughs and rolls his eyes. "Or start with some restaurants. You strike me as someone who lives on takeout and bad delivery."

She gives him a flat stare.

"Oh come on, you must know at least *one* person other than me. To start with, at least. If this stall you're talking about is off island, you're shit out of luck, but it's still a lead, right? And I can keep an eye out for your little twin."

Her breath catches. For a heartbeat, the room tilts, as if Soichi's presence doubles and another form stands just inside her peripheral vision. Then he pushes the drive toward her again, and the feeling passes.

Lena thanks him and as she leaves, he pipes up, loud enough for the front technician and waiting room to hear, "Goodbye, my criminal friend!"

Cheeks hot, she ducks her head, pretending not to hear him. As she walks to her bike, she rests a hand over her bag where the drive nests, and Soichi's suggestion circles in her mind. She hates the prospect of extra conversation, but the need to understand runs headlong into her resistance, and it won't release her even as the first warning gusts of the coming typhoon hit her.

With it, an idea pops up. There *is* one place that comes to mind.

FIVE

When Lena reaches the narrow strip of the lower quarter, most of its shops are dark, but partway down the block, one unit glows. The buildings on either side lean close, as though brick and concrete have curved themselves inward to keep the light. The restaurant's marquee is a beacon.

XIAO NO DLE HOUSE

Lena feathers her brakes, easing past and stopping in front of the closed store next door. She keeps the bike between herself and the restaurant like a pretense of a shield, a poor stand-in for concealment. She tells herself she shouldn't be here. Not before opening, not on a day off, and especially not with the drive in her sling, beating like a second pulse she can't ignore. She promises she'll leave. She'll push off, ride away, maybe laugh and treat this as a moment of impulse and nothing more.

Instead, she peeks through the window. Inside, someone moves with patient efficiency. Lena catches Runi's outline, hair twisted into that loose bun, her body inclined over the prep station. Even at this distance, even with glass between them, the flow of her motions holds Lena rapt, anchoring her in place.

A tightness cinches around her chest and doesn't release. What is she doing? She isn't thinking straight. This drive isn't her memory. It isn't Lena's feelings. She isn't supposed to want anything this much—not answers, clarity, or whatever this is gnawing at her. She's already broken rules and her reactions are unmoored, close to the surface threatening to break out. It's not safe, nor is it stable.

Her grip adjusts on the handlebars. She should leave. This is too much. She's off-balance. She pushes down on the pedal—

A lock clicks.

Lena freezes. The door opens behind her, and warm air wafts into the cool morning—ginger waking in oil and broth developing its backbone.

"Lena?"

She turns, caught mid-motion straddling the frame of her bike, leg and torso now at cringeworthy rotations and angles. Runi stands in the doorway, wiping her hands on a towel, one eyebrow creeping up as if the morning has suddenly become more interesting.

"You're early," she says.

Lena is grateful for the shadows as she tries to mask her ensuing gulp. She fixes her misaligned limbs.

"Well," Runi adds, stepping aside, "if you're lurking out here before I open, you might as well come in."

Lena waits for Runi to say or do something further, and when she doesn't, Lena clumsily hops off her bicycle and props it against the wall, kickstand into the same brick. She steps through the door behind Runi, eyes everywhere but the other woman, suddenly more awkward than usual. It's mildly short-lived as she intently takes in the shop's pre-opening calm: overheads set low, counters wiped down, and one pot heating on the back range. Nothing is staged yet, everything still in that half-hour before real work begins.

Runi slides past her, past the service divider, and heads to the shelves above the counter. Lena remains where she is, unsure whether to claim a stool or keep standing, hands hovering near the counter's edge.

"Let me guess—you're here for emergency packet noodles before I've even started the good batch." Runi's hand goes automatically to the familiar stack.

But Lena finds her voice just in time. "No. Um, no. Actually, I'm not here to eat."

Runi pauses and turns fully. Her hand drops. "Is everything okay?"

"Yeah! Fine!" It's too immediate and chipper. Quite unlike Lena. She starts, tries to elaborate, but nothing comes out. The drive presses into her breastbone, and the decision Lena had convinced herself she was ready for feels too real. She nods instead.

"Okay, so if it's not food, what brings the courier queen to my humble empire?"

Lena hesitates, but she's here now, already making a

fool of herself. She might as well ask the question, even if it's absurd. "You...know a lot of kitchens in Meiyu, right?"

Runi's brow rises while the other pinches down. "The way you say it—is that a compliment or an accusation?"

Lena freezes. Again.

But Runi only chuckles and flutters her fingers.

"Right. Um, I'm trying to find one. Old, maybe small. They make cōng yóu bǐng. Egg and chili crisp on top. Maybe some basil." Lena falters, aware of how strangely specific and also generic that sounds. "It's for a project."

"I can make you some if you'd like," Runi offers. "I've got most of the ingredients. Don't have basil on hand though."

"No." The word exits sharper than Lena intends. "Sorry, I mean—I'm looking for a place that makes them."

Runi studies her. "Okay. A place." She brushes a crumb off the countertop. "You know cōng yóu bǐng is on half the island's menus, yeah?"

Lena waves her hands, trying again. "It'd be a night market stall. That only does that—cōng yóu bǐng." She doesn't recall anything else on the flat-top grill.

Runi's eyebrow climbs again. "Only that?" She suppresses a snort and smiles. "A specialty place, then. You know *I* specialize, too, right?" Her grin widens. "Lena, do you think all of us food-industry folk gather once a week to swap notes and business cards? Because I hate to disappoint you—"

Lena's shoulders sag.

"Oh, no, I'm just giving you a hard time." Runi laughs, but not unkindly. She continues, "I actually can think of a few. You don't see too many of those anymore—specializing, I mean." She squeezes her mouth to the side. "Hm, there was a stall in the East Market that did basil and egg on theirs. It might still be around, might not. A family cart near Harbor Gate, but they were pretty seasonal, I think. And up by Memorial Road? A couple used to run a stand. Good one, too. Long lines in the mornings...*and* nights."

Runi pauses, fingertips resting at the dimple just below her lips. Lena follows the gesture to a small beauty mark she's never noticed before on the woman's neck. She promptly averts her gaze.

Okay. Three options. It's more than what she had before—which was nothing. That's a start.

Lena finds her voice. "Do you remember what they looked like?"

"Oh, you're making me work!" Runi chuckles, then shrugs. "Depends on which one. It's been some time since I've wandered the markets, but let's see... East had a big steel plate and those tiny plastic stools everyone hates—too short, terrible for the knees. Flimsy, too." She shudders and continues, "Harbor Gate's cart was under a giant blue, no—green tarp with this bell that rang every time someone bumped into it. And the Memorial Road one..." Her face scrunches up and she squints at nothing in particular. "A few metal stools, maybe a hand-painted sign?"

Something in Lena sinks. None of these descriptions sits quite right. Close, but not exact enough.

Runi keeps going, now almost to herself. "In weather like this? You could smell the griddles a block away. Rain hits the hot oil every now and then and everything just... blossoms. The whole street smells like onion and salted dough."

Lena's breath stutters. The memory and emotion—the ones that aren't hers—flare. She recognizes that. She *remembers* that. She knows it in a way she shouldn't.

"I...I thought I imagined that part."

"Hm?"

Lena shakes her head.

"You've got that look again," Runi murmurs.

"What look?"

"The one people get when they're lost. Or wandered off. Not in a bad way." Runi smiles. "You have it quite a bit when you're here."

Heat rushes into Lena's face. She focuses on the rack of packaged noodles instead of Runi's eyes. "I don't know what you mean."

"Sure you don't," Runi teases. She sweeps the towel along the counter. "Well, if you find this stall, whichever one you're hunting, let me know. I haven't had good cōng yóu bǐng in ages." Her voice lilts. "And I wouldn't object to a stroll in the market—with the right company."

Lena's throat constricts and she tries to swallow. She forces herself to nod, grateful and mortified in equal measure. "Thank you."

"That's all you came for? Interrogating me on bǐng and every kitchen I've ever known? Should I be jealous?" Runi flashes a grin. "You sure you don't want something to eat?"

"No." Lena steps back. "Really, I should go."

Runi exhales, a small sound of concession. "Then at

least be careful out there. The weather service says the typhoon's supposed to make landfall early. Streets flood fast in this part of town."

Lena mumbles another thanks, drawn forward by the impatient urge that has nothing to do with hunger and everything to do with the stall, the unknown owner of that joy, and the reason they surrendered it. She heads for the door. As she steps into the damp morning, Runi calls after her, not loudly or insistently, but enough to catch.

"Hey, if you need help searching, I can have Emery cover for me."

The door shuts.

Rain falls in an unbroken run, too mild to empty the streets but persistent enough to soak anything that stays. It beads along canopies and windows, blurring the glow of bright neon signs over the market. Umbrellas bloom and fold with the occasional gust, and dark shapes weave intermittently between closed arcades and stands hawking food, clothing, or trinkets. The smell of wet fabric and stewed vegetables, skewers, and noodles on steel trays floats through Lena's senses.

Under a sagging Halcyon sign reminding the city of monthly credits, she parks her bicycle and yanks her poncho hood closer around her face. She slips under the first row of tarps, shoes skimming over trickles on the pavement. The precipitation has elevated its tempo, an insistent drumming she feels in the hinge of her jaw. Lena scans the strip. Stalls that might open later won't bother once the heavier downpour sets in. If she's going to find what she's tracking down, it has to happen now.

She starts with the place Runi mentioned first, and the East Market stand is easy to spot. Blue tarp, wide steel griddle, and stacks of the little plastic stools. The vendor is there working, patting and flipping scallion pancakes in quick practiced arcs. The gray hair under a bucket hat estimates the right age for the possible owner of an old-generation drive. Within a few steps of the cart, the scent hits her. Sesame oil, scallion, and crisp dough.

But wrong. Too heavy. Too fried. Too…loud. It's wetter here than in the memory, but that's not what's off.

Lena watches the vendor fold an egg into the dough and press the sleeve between his palms. Every movement tells her this isn't it. The pacing, the environment, the inward pinch in her gut, none of it matches. She turns away and moves on.

Harbor Gate lies farther out. By the time Lena rides up to it, the squall has intensified, blowing sideways through the channels underneath fixed and temporary overhangs. The kind of weather that shuts the majority of the island's stalls before they can finish heating their pans. Whatever window she's chasing today has exponentially shrunk.

But she finds it. Or at least what Runi's described. The cart sits dormant under a green canvas, its bell clinking each time the wind lifts a corner. The printed sign hangs crooked beside it, chipped and faded. A few overturned crates and a shuttered fryer are tucked underneath. Lena steps closer. There's no fresh scent of dough hitting oil. Nothing to match what she felt. She'll have to circle back.

As she rides toward Memorial Road, time billows and the storm worsens. Sheets cascade across asphalt, fast and slanted, thunderous enough to wreck her sense of direction. Headlights smear into long starbursts, white halos expanding across her vision. She blinks hard, but the glare lingers, brightening the edges of everything. Without warning, her tires lose grip. The back wheel skids and her heart kicks hard. Lena braces, breath clipped short. Another gust shoves at her side and she overcorrects, handlebars juddering in her hands. Everything piles on: engines, splashes, horns, the slap of tires through puddles. Too many directions. Too much input. The wrong kind of noise.

So Lena narrows her world to the white line along the road, riding near but not on it, hyperaware of drivers that might not see her in time. Her neck and shoulders knot until they cramp, and she forces air into her lungs then out, trying to coax her diaphragm, but her muscles refuse to loosen.

As she hits the next stretch, relief comes, and everything nearly recedes as she enters a tangle of tarps. She continues on Memorial Road where vendors drag coverings into place with resigned movements. Here, a handful of stalls are stubbornly in operation while others remain folded into skeletons of metal poles and plastic siding, still compact in their refusal to open.

Lena finds her footing, parks, and takes in the row. Lamps flare under the strain of the storm, and a couple of vendors bow over prep bowls, slicing vegetables with weary but measured rhythm. The place isn't completely empty of customers, but the lack is noticeable. She lets the spike of panic pass and scans her surroundings. She expects scallion and oil to flare, but underneath the partial cover, the air lies strained and stuffy instead. As Lena adjusts, she focuses and separates what she can smell: that unmistakable sour-fermented brine from a stinky tofu stand, ginger from a noodle pot, and something sugary and sweet from a confection store.

She walks the length of the market once. Then a second time. She stops in front of an empty space where a stand might've once stood; the only thing left is a plastic sign hanging from a wire, its face bleached by weather and time. She waits for a minute, though she doesn't know for what.

Her attention turns to where a nearby vendor is frying *jī pái*.[1] The chicken cutlets have been pounded flat as a Halcyon affect drive, dredged in spiced flour, and lowered into a shallow vat of oil. The stall, little more than a metal cart sheltered beneath a bowing vinyl cover, is lit by a single bulb that dangles from a cord, casting a tight pocket of light over the work surface. Oil snaps in bursts and the crisping batter spits up pepper and starch that seem to float before they fall back into the space.

Lena's gut constricts. It's the wrong food, the wrong stand, but the noise scratches at a hollow place inside her. When the vendor glances up, Lena steps forward and starts to raise two fingers, then drops one. She doesn't need more, her eyes just think she does.

The vendor scoops a cutlet from the oil, lays it on a wire rack where the excess runs off in shimmering rivulets. Its surface is blistered to a deep gold, edges curling where the sizzling heat has caught them. He wraps it in paper and asks about spice. Lena nods. He dusts it with chili powder and white pepper from tin containers and passes it across with a warning about both heats. She taps her handheld against the worn-out scanner.

Then, Lena sits at one of the metal square tables behind the cart, positions a second stool close, and takes the large breaded chicken fillet in both hands. The first bite cracks and breaks between her teeth; the crust gives way to meat that's juicy and steaming, spices budding slow along her tongue. She hadn't noticed how empty her stomach was. The search has carved away the day, and though she's passed stalls of sausages, tofu, oyster pancakes, and more, she's been too focused to stop and eat. Now that she has, she pays attention. Salt. Pepper. Crispy batter. The meat, its exterior, all of it is good.

She settles into each bite and her attention simultaneously sharpens and softens to the scene around her. The market is far from busy, but it still buzzes, reined in by weather and the hour. Voices trade short orders, food couriers collect boxed and bagged meals, and a peddler's child laughs as they try to balance on a crate. Deeper down the row, a wok scrapes across a burner, followed by the sudden roar of gas catching. Trays knock together as they're stacked for a dinner rush that may not arrive.

At the fringe of Lena's sight, movement stirs. Two men duck under the neighboring tarp, shaking water from their collars and sleeves as they slide onto stools, probably come straight from the office.

"Told her to go to the clinic this week," one says

loudly. "I went yesterday. Took the edge right off and I'm sleeping better again."

The other one agrees. "Quick fix. Worth it."

Their voices dissolve into the squawk and chatter of an electronic store's loudspeaker, and Lena disregards both noises. Nothing in this market has risen to meet what she seeks. She could wait here or ride the long route back to Harbor Gate to see if the other cart with its little bell is open yet, but she doesn't want to deal with the storm any more than she has to. Especially not another replay of the chaos on the slick roads.

As she resigns into a decision, she lets her focus uncoil again. Lena has sat in this market before. Not on this stool and not for this reason, but the posture fits too easily, as if her body and its motions remember more than she does. The sensation stays at the border of awareness, present but dulled, like something wrapped in gauze.

She chews a little more of the cutlet. She could finish —the hunger is there—but she slows. The flavor and textures are all present but something doesn't quite resolve. Lena studies the paper between her fingers and watches the oil stains mottle in uneven blotches, a map with no legend, small islands merging together.

She doesn't know how long she stares, but she finally folds the wrapper around what food remains and stands. A nearby bin claims the leftovers with a thud. A waste, in more ways than one. She brushes her hands clean and heads toward the corner, where a small tea shop refuses to submit to the weather.

"One hot," Lena says. Her fingers almost mark out a second.

The vendor ladles *năi chá*[2] from a large steel pot into a paper cup, seals a lid, and sets it between them. Lena curls her fingers around it, and the heat bleeds into her skin, verging on a burn she forces herself to hold. A mild, creamy sweetness rises, woody and delicate, cutting through the sharper scents of fried batter still clinging to her hair and clothes.

She doesn't drink it yet. Cup in hand, Lena walks the row again, and the stands and shops fade behind light curtains of rain as she approaches the end. The puddles in the dark pavement brighten and gather her reflection, stretched and bent by each passing ripple. For a second, she sees two shapes in the distorted outline—one a half-step behind the other—but it's only water shifting with the wind.

When the beverage no longer scalds her fingers, Lena takes a sip. The first draw is silken and semi-sweet. Warmth travels down her throat and eddies in the cavity of her core. Like the jī pái, the milk tea doesn't exactly open anything inside her, but it doesn't slide off entirely, either. By the time she returns to her flat, the milk tea has cooled, forgotten in her bicycle basket. She hasn't finished it.

SIX

"You're off tempo."

Lena startles and straightens. "Sorry?"

Behind the counter, Mr. Peng watches her over the top rim of his glasses. He drums the stylus against his tablet screen. "You scanned that code twice. And you didn't check the seal on the packet before it."

"Oh." Her head empties as she scrambles to regain her composure. "I didn't sleep well." It touches close enough to the truth.

He doesn't comment, simply gives her a long look, enough that she feels the piercing assessment in it. "Storm's shifting," he says at last. "Pressure's dropped early. People get unfocused when the weather's like this."

"I'm fine," she says automatically.

"Mm." Mr. Peng sets his stylus down. "If you need adjustment, go to the clinic. But notify me first so I can change your schedule."

"I don't need one."

"Most people who *do* say that," he replies. It's delivered the same way he notes inventory or equipment faults: routine and factual. He glances toward the open bay door. The horizon has already darkened another shade. "Stay off the lower roads on your way home tonight. They'll flood."

"Yes, sir."

He adds, almost as an afterthought: "We have the car outside. You should really consider taking it. That bike won't do you any favors."

Lena is uncertain if he expects an answer. By the time she thinks to add anything, Mr. Peng has turned back to his annotations.

She takes up the previous sleeve she overlooked, but pauses. Her hands seem steady enough, but she's been out of sorts since the previous night, *definitely* since the defective drive. Possibly even before that.

Stops blend together and Lena's certain each task is done correctly—or close enough that her armband doesn't squeeze, that no angry alerts appear. She's on time despite the weather, despite reading and rereading addresses, or standing too long at lockers and kiosks. More than once she catches herself listening for a sound or raising her nose for a scent that never presents itself. At a mid-route intersection, a billboard depicting a beaming family bears down on her, shouting Halcyon's morning message—*Balance earns trust. Balance earns stability.* But the text passes across her field of view without catching, as if it's meant for someone else.

Her route runs in a wider loop and she misses lunch without meaning to—forced into a mandated break. Lena only wants the shift behind her. Her handheld pings reminders that she swipes away on reflex, her mind already drifting ahead. By the time her final delivery is complete, she's not far from Harbor Gate, and the air has that misleading chill that suggests the evening might clear. However, she knows better; it's a false front, and the worst part is rolling in. She should head home, but instead she angles her bike and empty bag toward the market road.

And this time, Harbor Gate is alive, taking advantage of the brief weather lull. Stalls throw color onto the darkening street, and tarps ripple gently overhead. Lena goes straight to the stand she saw the previous day, and this time the tarp is rolled back, the griddle warmed up. A young man with a bright-green apron dances through his setup.

Lena stops a few paces away.

Dough. Scallion. Egg. Even the colorful green of basil. The overall shape matches what she remembers.

But the rest doesn't. The vendor's spatula strikes the griddle in beats too slow. The oil doesn't sing the way it should. As she steps closer, the scent leans toward smoke, almost charred, instead of the clear edge of something she can't name but still expects. Even the stacked paper sleeves are different, printed with red cranes instead of plain white.

Those details shouldn't automatically disqualify the experience, since the affect drive's memory is from another time. A different paper sleeve could be part of the market's change, a different generation, but it altogether feels like another stall. The mismatch twists her stomach.

It isn't her emotion or her memory. Lena knows that. She shouldn't be out here chasing a stranger's moment, someone else's beatitude. The whole thing is foolish, but the wanting and need to fill that gap doesn't ease.

When the young man cocks a questioning brow, Lena shakes her head and backs away, apology written in the dip of her shoulders. She finds her way back to her bicycle, breathing around the disappointment.

As she turns toward home, she thinks about the drive, about replaying the colorful images, the warmth and buoyancy, all of it, even in its deteriorating state. And then after her mind swirls too much and Lena's taken a second wrong turn, she cuts the thought down. She's aware of the gravity, of how badly she wants to hang on.

The ride home stretches, and by the time she's at her building, evening has congealed into a strange desolation. Lena parks her bike and steps into the stairwell. She climbs a single flight when a screen door creaks above her.

Mrs. Kuan's voice floats down, greeting her with that misplaced name again, voice warm with a puzzled note. A head peeks over the banister, disappears, and then her neighbor steps into view, a watering can hooked over her wrist, dripping on the landing. Purple reading glasses hang from a delicate chain around her neck, catching a sliver of light. "You look run down," she says. "Too many days of this strange weather?"

Lena exhales as she continues up the stairs. "Just a long shift." She squeezes by the woman, who doesn't seem to realize she's standing in the middle of the path.

Mrs. Kuan croons, unconvinced. "The rain is something awful. Cover up—and properly! You'll get sick!" She bats lightly at Lena's elbow. "And you come over if you need something hot. I've got tea ready."

Lena makes a noncommittal sound, but pauses at the first step past the landing, waiting for anything else. A noncommittal politeness.

"You haven't stopped by in a while."

Lena tenses. She's never intentionally stopped by at all. She's especially never been inside her neighbor's flat. "Thank you, but I just need to get upstairs," she manages.

Mrs. Kuan purses her lips and hums again, but doesn't insist further. And with that, Lena takes the opening and quickly escapes to her floor, unlocks her door, and steps into the flat's dimness. The place feels duller, emptier than when she left it. She sets her helmet down and goes straight to her room where she takes her time and changes. Then she returns to the kitchen and starts the kettle.

Meanwhile, the draw of the copied drive is impossible to ignore. She considers playing it again, even knowing the duplicate has lost too much, knowing what she initially felt has eroded. The happiness, the memory fragments are intact, but the texture, what makes it real— if it ever was real—is wearing away, thinning like cloth handled too often.

While her tea's steeping, Lena sits on the edge of her bed, elbows on her knees, face in her hands, trying to breathe the agitation down. The leads she had for the drive's owner have fizzled out. She's not sure what else she can do.

Then comes a knock.

Through her fingers, Lena peeks an eye out. The drive stares back at her.

The knock comes again. Soft but persistent.

After another pause, Lena trudges to the front door and peers through the peephole. Her lips press together in a thin line and she pulls it open.

"Mrs. Kuan?" Lena has never seen her neighbor anywhere but the second floor.

The woman leans against the banister, breath still raspy. "I made too much," Mrs. Kuan announces, as if that explains everything. "And it's no good eating alone. Come down."

"Oh, thank you, but I—"

"Just for a few minutes."

The drive is losing definition by the day, if not by the hour, and Lena wants to close the door and replay what little she can, clutch at whatever she can, before it fades further. "I—really, I'm fine," she says.

Mrs. Kuan tuts and peers at her over her purple glasses. "'Fine' is what people say right before they topple over. Come now. Humor an old woman. I shouldn't be climbing all these stairs, anyway." She hikes one foot up a few centimeters and makes a pained face. "I'll snap in half."

Lena blinks. Her neighbor's statement and expression

wavers somewhere between absurd and earnest. She holds back a deep sigh.

"Okay," she concedes. "Let me help you." She steps forward, bare feet against cold landing, before she's fully realized she's been played.

Mrs. Kuan's features change immediately—smug—and she takes Lena's arm with a grip stronger than expected, locking her to her side. Together, they make measured progress down the stairs (although Lena's positive the old woman is overexaggerating her lean into her). Mrs. Kuan mutters about her joints, the weather, and the foolishness of a building with no reliable elevator.

Inside the second-floor flat, Lena's met with the whiff of deep soy sauce, savory fat, floral perfume, and linen dried indoors. A kettle whistles on the stove—an old thing, far older than Mrs. Kuan. Lena stands awkwardly in the kitchen until the old woman prods and waves her to the adjoining dining and living room. The furniture is old but orderly, arranged with the care of habit rather than for visitors. On the accent table sits a photo. Lena doesn't mean to stare, but something about its composition holds her: a young boy and girl, shoulder to shoulder, laughing at something outside the frame. She pauses again and something inside her turns.

"My children," Mrs. Kuan says. She remains next to the stove, tending to the kettle. "When they were wee things, they used to drag me through every market on this island every chance they'd get. Always after a different food or flavor of the week, month, sometimes even a year! Stubborn creatures, those two. Always together. You couldn't bring one anywhere without the other."

Pressure spreads at Lena's side, the way a thumb might find an old bruise. She swallows. "What...What kind of food?"

"Oh, whatever phase they were into at the time. Some months it was skewers and buns. Some seasons sweet tofu. And for a while"—Mrs. Kuan chuckles—"they hunted for the perfect bǐng. Said they'd know it by the smell alone."

Lena's pulse stirs and her head pulls up. "Bǐng?"

"*Zhuā bǐng,*[1] *dà bǐng,*[2] dàn bǐng, cōng yóu bǐng—"

"Did they ever find it—cōng yóu bǐng? Do you remember which market and stall?"

Mrs. Kuan only hums. Her back is turned.

"Auntie. The market? Stall?"

"Hm? Oh, whichever one had a line that day. Children don't care too much about specifics. Only the treat at the end." When she faces Lena, she has two full bowls in her hands. "What are you doing standing there? Sit! Sit!"

Lena obeys, and as Mrs. Kuan sets the bowl in front of her, she catches sight of a slew of photos and papers held in place under the transparent tablecloth.

"You're bone and shadows. Eat before you disappear."

When Lena doesn't move, the old woman nudges the dish closer. Steam rises from the *lǔ ròu fàn,*[3] braised pork belly glossy over rice. Lena's eyes, then nose, latch on immediately. Five spice and rounded, rendered, and caramelized pork fat. Her stomach growls.

"Eat!"

As Mrs. Kuan sets her own bowl down, then fetches the teapot and two cups, Lena digs in. She takes a bite, a good mix of rice and meat carrying salt and sweetness in equal measure. The soy sauce lays down a foundation mellowed by sugar that never quite announces itself. The spices, star anise and shallot, bloom. Fat, sauce, and meat seep into the rice, grain by grain, each mouthful unified, inseparable as if the dish has erased the idea of components altogether. The richness catches her off guard, but something eases. It orients her toward the bowl, toward the old woman, away from the fixation of the drive, of everything else waiting upstairs.

Mrs. Kuan pours tea, humming tunelessly, her own rice and pork still untouched. "People think memories are tidy things," she starts, "but the things we care about shift. They wander. Change shape. Sometimes we recall the food and forget the place. Sometimes the place outgrows the people. We don't always know why we hold on to one piece or why we let go of another."

Lena's fingers tense against warm porcelain and her gaze slides back to the framed photo. She isn't exactly sure where Mrs. Kuan's words are heading—if they have any direction at all.

Her neighbor tuts and waves a hand as if she's read Lena's mind. "Ignore an old woman's rambling. Tell me about your day instead. Was it really so long?"

Lena opens her mouth, closes it, opens it again. How can she explain a day spent chasing something that isn't hers? Something that feels as though it matters even though it doesn't? It won't leave her alone. Or *she* won't leave it alone. She's not sure which. She takes a deep breath and settles on, "I didn't find what I was looking for."

Mrs. Kuan nods and sips her tea. "Then you'll look

again tomorrow. That's what the living do. We keep going toward the next moment. Even if we don't know why yet. We persist."

Lena doesn't know how to add on to that, so she bows her head and eats while Mrs. Kuan continues, talking about the neighborhood, the crack in one of the steps, the neighbor who keeps overwatering their plants. It's ordinary conversation, but it fills the room. Lena catches herself leaning forward, listening, actually enjoying herself.

Later, when she returns upstairs, her shirt smelling of clove and spices, the old current of anxiety, guilt, and fear rises in the face of the drive's flickering blue indicator. But now something sits differently, quieter. The echo of a shared meal clings to Lena, and the evening's warmth rests. Even though the drive is still on its decline and she's no nearer to the cōng yóu bǐng, the stall, or the owner.

For the first time that day, she feels something close to relief.

NEW MESSAGE
HALCYON INTEGRATED WELLNESS

Hi Lena, this is your monthly reminder from Halcyon Integrated Wellness. Please confirm your appointment for an Emotional Unburdening Protocol appointment in three days at 7:00 PM at the Halcyon Balance Center District 3 location. Appointments must be confirmed by 12:00 PM the day prior to your appointment to avoid cancellation fees. Please reply "1" to confirm or "2" to reschedule. We look forward to servicing you. Thank you.

Hello Lena, please confirm your appointment in two days at 7:00 PM at the District 3 location. Please reply "1" to confirm or "2" to reschedule. Thank you.

SEVEN

By midmorning, Lena's route bends earlier than usual toward the lower district. An unscheduled request after her second stop shuffles her sequence and sends her on a downhill detour. If possible, most people avoid this area when storms build. Rain is already slating down, and the drains choke and croak as they give up on the day.

Lena rides carefully, lifting her feet when her wheels slice through deep channels. Her poncho keeps her shoulders dry, but water has soaked her socks and the cuffs of her pants. She knows logically she should have taken the depot vehicle—Mr. Peng had hinted again—but like every other time, she'd brushed the suggestion away.

Buildings huddle overhead as gutters below spit streams that stitch along the pavement. Lena's last delivery was streets back, and the next is up toward the mid-terrace. She should have taken the last intersection and angled away to a higher road, given the floods a wider berth, but then she sees it.

Xiao Noodle House sits in the worst part of the dip, a tier of sandbags stacked like a low buttress in front of its door. Each time the street water swells, a slick tongue squeezes over the top. And just inside, Runi is dragging a mop in sharp strokes trying to stem the tide with middling success. Metal stools sit upside down on the counter, and crates of dried goods and ingredients are stacked on higher surfaces along with any fixtures that can be hoisted beyond the water's advance.

Before she thinks it through, Lena squeezes her brakes. Her back tire skids, sending a fan of water over her already soaked shoes. Her bike comes to a halt beside a recycling bin pinned against a clogged curb drain, turning as the runoff pushes against it.

She shouldn't stop, but she casts her eyes across the road again. A sheet of water sluices past the sandbags, past the door, and spreads over tile. Sleeves rolled high, Runi plants her feet and shoves it back, jaw set, a determined snarl on her face. Lena can't hear what Runi is saying, but the cook's lips are sharp in a motion and form meant for harsh sentiments.

Lena's grip locks on the handlebars. She could ride on. She *should*. That would be normal. That would be routine. And like a reminder, her armband gives a small buzz. Her next checkpoint and delivery awaits. But Lena stands there, one shoe submerged, watching Runi inside battle the floodwater.

A weight inside her tilts, rolling toward an edge. Maybe it's the pull left over from the defective drive.

Maybe it's the way the copied version on her desk flickered last night. Maybe it's the feeling she still can't name, something that ought to mean more than it does, hovering just out of reach. Whatever it is, it keeps her here.

Lena walks her bike through ankle-high water and wedges it into a narrow space where she trusts it won't get swept away. She unhooks the courier bag from the back mount and heaves its strap over her head. Cold presses into her feet, and her toes have gone completely numb. She gingerly steps over the drenched sandbags, eases the door open just enough, and slips through the narrow gap.

The chime goes off.

Surprised, Runi jerks up. She pushes damp hair off her temples with the back of her wrist. "Oh thank god you're here, Emery."

Lena's used to being mistaken for someone else.

"It's been—" Runi's eyes flutter up along with her hand. "Oh. Lena? What are you—are you delivering in this?"

"Do you need help?" Lena asks, ignoring the question. She steps past the shop owner and sets her courier bag in the cradle of an upturned stool.

Runi turns with her, feet still rooted. She shakes her head and checks the mop in her hands, at the persistent creep of water edging under the door into the shop. "I mean—yes. Badly." A short breath escapes her, equal parts laughter and frustration. "But you're working."

"What do you need me to do?" Lena pulls her poncho over her head. She would've taken it off earlier, but it doesn't seem to matter much with how slick the ground already is inside.

Runi starts to protest, but Lena only brushes past the woman again. She hooks her garment next to the window and out of the way. When she turns, Runi's mouth is slightly agape, attention caught as Lena ties her hair back with a band she's plucked from her still-worn sling.

Runi closes her mouth, and then drags a second bucket past the divider. "Here," she says. "This cursed street drain. I would've had an extra set of hands, but I think Emery and his daughter are trapped across the island. He was bringing more sandbags!"

Lena takes the pail, and heads to the doorway. The water isn't deep, but it keeps pooling faster than the small line of defense outside the door can hold. And on the street, the whole row has turned out. The shopkeeper across the way kneels in the entrance with a teenager, pushing water away together with plastic dustpans. Farther down, three workers congregate over a drain with a length of bamboo, poking and stabbing at whatever's choking it. The typhoon has everyone occupied.

Inside, she and Runi fall into rhythm together—Runi drawing water toward the door, Lena carrying load after load to the curb and tossing it into the overrun gutter. Between motions, Lena tugs off her chest rig and armband and hangs both on a rung above the Halcyon bag. To her side, Runi sweeps the mop, eyebrows furrowing when the armband gives an angry vibration against the stool's leg.

"Aren't you supposed to be on your route," Runi says more than asks. "I don't want to get you in trouble."

Lena dismisses the concern with a quiet grunt and busies herself by filling the next bucket. The water just won't stop, and her attempts to fix the height of the sandbags is limited by their current resources. So, they keep at it. Runi mopping while Lena collects and dumps. They switch when Lena's back starts to ache, and continue on. It's tedious, repetitive work. The kind that compresses time. And after a long stretch, either by the success of the people outside or some mercy the rain grants, the incoming water slows, even recedes. The shop's tiles lose their sheen.

"Better," Runi says, throwing the last cloth inside her pail. "Not great, but better." She blows a lock of hair from her eyes. "You didn't have to do all this."

"You needed an extra pair of hands." Lena leans the mop against the window and steps away from the door. Her socks squish in her shoes. Pins and needles race along her fingers as she claps her hands together and waits for feeling to return.

"Sure," Runi says, watching her a beat longer than necessary. "And thank you, sincerely, but you still didn't have to."

Lena rolls a shoulder. She doesn't know how long she's been there, and she still hasn't worked out how to explain the instinct that made her stop.

"Let me get towels down before someone breaks their neck. *That* would really ruin the day."

Runi disappears behind the counter into the back, leaving Lena standing in the middle of their hard-won battle. While she waits, Lena breathes in the shop's familiar mix—ginger and broth—although now it's mixed with the smells of heavy weather and wet wood. A patch lights up on her sling bag—her handheld—but she diverts her attention back to the quiet shop around her. It's so unlike the usual setup she's used to. Not bad, just naked in a way. But no less warming. Her focus cuts out as Runi returns with an armful of towels. Together, she and Lena lay them over the worst spots, pressing out what moisture is left.

"I guess these storms remind you where the leaks really are." Runi eyes the front of the shop. She chuffs. "I could be a poet. Or a plumber." She then pokes a floor fan into place, but leaves it unplugged, studying the wall outlet with narrowed suspicion. Her hands settle at her hips. "So. Crisis mostly handled. You should probably get going before the next wave hits. Especially before the road turns into a river again."

Lena glances outside. The water level has dropped a bit, but the rain hasn't eased. She wipes her palms on her pants. "My next stop isn't urgent." Not entirely true. "I can stay a bit. If the water comes back in, you shouldn't have to handle it alone."

Runi chuckles, a huffed breath that sounds both amused and relieved. "You might be the only person I've met who volunteers for extra work."

"I'm already here," Lena says with a shrug.

"That's your reasoning?" Runi arches an eyebrow. "Terrible logic, but I'm not going to argue with it anymore. I'll take it. I love good company." She moves back behind the counter and surveys her prep station— cutting board halfway out, knives in the rack, and green vegetables stacked on the stove and sink. "What a mess," she mutters. "Didn't finish a single chore this morning. This damn storm chewed right through my plans, and from the state of all this and all that"—she gestures outside—"it might take another day or two to recover. What a waste."

Runi lets out a tremendous sigh, then rummages along the upper shelf. She fetches two familiar red-and-white packets, and gently thumps them onto the counter. "Lucky I have these. You hungry?"

"I'm fine," Lena says, but she drifts closer, median between them.

"You're always fine," Runi replies, although without any real bite. She wiggles a finger at one of the stools. "If you're staying, sit for a moment."

"You don't have to—"

"I'm feeding me." Runi tears open a packet. "This defense has me famished, and I'll need reserves if I'm to keep this tantrum of weather away. And you?" She picks up the second packet, fingers primed to pinch it open.

Lena concedes with a nod.

Runi grins and pries the plastic seam apart. "You? You're a bonus." Her teeth bite into her lower lip, smile still in her eyes as she fills the kettle. She then taps the outlet with the tip of her finger. Its light stays on. "At least the power's still with us. That's a small miracle. Unless it decides to fry us in the next few minutes." Runi's brows furrow for a second, but then they relax as she laughs.

Lena's mouth turns up at the corners.

While the water heats, Runi glances at the Halcyon bag. "I've been wondering about this for a while and I guess now's just as good a time to ask... Do you really haul all your deliveries in that?" She pauses briefly, then continues, "Feels...archaic. Same with that two-wheeler of yours—no offense. Day like this, you're practically swimming deliveries across the district."

Lena adjusts the bag on the stool. She doesn't bother with her armband or sling pack, both of which have surprisingly fallen quiet. Then she realizes Runi's watching her, waiting. "Oh." She gives a weak shrug. "It's part of the job."

"Well, that much I figured," Runi teases as she prepares two bowls, one of them Lena's chipped blue. "You're out here almost every day, always on that bike, but what are you carting around? You never say."

Lena's actually never talked this long with the owner-cook before. Not until the other day. And now. "Drives. Affect drives," she answers, pulling down a stool.

Runi's eyebrows rise. "Oh, so you are with Halcyon?"

Lena nods.

"Huh. I had no idea those things traveled around like mail." She flutters a finger toward the bag. "So what's in them? People's...feelings, right? How does that even work?" She shakes her head. "Why?"

"It's protocol. Affect tags need physical transfer."

"You'd think by now everything's floating in some cloud network."

"Certain affects don't hold shape in wireless transit. Signals pick up interference, electrical noise, humidity, grid congestion—you know, there're too many variables. The patterns deform. Emotions get scrambled and physical drives keep the neural impression stable. Without the proper maintenance, you get attenuation.

Breakup and degradation." Lena stops herself and stares at the kettle, then at the wall behind Runi. She's overexplaining and talking far too much. She clears her throat.

But Runi leans back, her hip against the back counter, eyes gleaming. Her nose wrinkles. "So...you carry people's emotions around. In a bag."

"Yes."

Runi's finger swoops in a little halo. "In this kind of weather."

"The drives are sealed."

"No backups? Or a safety net?"

"There can be, but the primary imprint has to be moved by hand. Copies don't hold as long or well. They break down without the proper care." Lena winces at the reminder of the fading file in her flat.

Runi is quiet, gaze on her.

Heat rises under Lena's collar, and she quickly diverts her attention back to the wall.

"So technical," Runi murmurs. "You sound like someone who does more than just carry packages around."

Lena swallows. She doesn't offer to explain the demotion.

"But..." Runi adds, "it still sounds like plenty to trust in typhoons and bicycles."

There's nothing Lena can think of to respond.

Thankfully, the kettle clicks off, and Runi moves forward. She pours boiling water over the noodles, covers the bowls with plates, and drums her fingers over each one as if urging them along. "So," she says after another lull, "did you find it? That cōng yóu bǐng you were chasing."

Lena stares at the plate edges, imagining the steam trying to escape and curl past. "No."

Runi makes a sound of resigned acknowledgment. "Hm. Figures. Markets don't stay the same. Blink twice and something you loved turns into a mass-market tornado potato stand or an oversauced corndog counter."

Lena nods. "The ones you mentioned, they felt…close, but wrong. All of them." She can feel Runi studying her—really studying her. She doesn't dare look up.

"That's okay, though, right?" When Lena doesn't offer more, Runi traces a finger around one of the plates and continues. "I get it. The strange part is that 'wrong'—those off notes tend to stick—sometimes more than 'right' does."

"What do you mean?"

"Well, you'd know better than I do. With Halcyon, I mean. You probably see it all the time. Sure, we all try to stick to the maintenance schedule—maybe not me, I'm *terrible* at keeping track." Runi chuffs. "But people don't miss their appointments when something 'wrong' happens. You don't miss those. *Those* 'flaws' stand out. It's why we do it, right?" Runi removes the plates and passes the blue bowl over the median. "I clipped something big once. A few years back. Went to the clinic like everyone else. Signed the forms, did the counseling session, picked the neat little package of 'relief from prolonged distress.' They made it all sound so tidy." A chuckle slips out.

Lena's pulse jumps. "What did you clip?"

Runi reaches over, opens the chopstick box, hands one

set to Lena, and gathers another for herself. She stirs her noodles. "Long story. Ugly ending." She shrugs. "But it was good, getting rid of the way it felt. God, that terrible pit in my stomach when I walked past the places we used to go, that knot in my heart every time I pictured her. I'd feel so sick."

"Her?" Lena asks before she can stop herself.

"Ex." Runi shrugs again. "We were foolish and stupid for a few years. Then we were mean. I figured cutting the ache out would give me back the parts that weren't ruined."

"Did it?"

"In some ways." Runi stares at Lena's bowl, at the chip on its rim. "I can still recall every detail. The way she chopped garlic, the way she'd steal the best bits out of the pot and *think* I didn't notice. And the way she walked out." Her lip twitches. "All of it's there. But there's nothing under it. No punch or sting. It's like reading an old menu from a place I never sat down in."

Runi quiets, and steam dampens Lena's face as she blows into the broth. The smell of the powdered broth is evanescent; its flavor never quite arrives.

"I used to have another dish on the board," Runi goes on. "Actually, it's one her father helped me get right—the balance of sauce and vinegar, the right heat from the garlic... People ordered it all the time, and I loved making it, but after I clipped, I couldn't get it right anymore. I'd use the same ingredients, the same timing. I could follow the recipe down to every little detail, and it came out fine. Just...different. Off by a hair." Her noodles sit untouched.

"I took it off the menu. Funny how that works." Runi

sets her chopsticks on the rim of her bowl. "The clinic gave me those options: sell, archive, or dispose. I told them to archive it—probably me being a coward, too afraid to make an actual decision at the time." She shrugs. "So it's probably still sitting in some vault somewhere with a tidy little label." She curves her hand and swipes it through the air like an invisible sign. "'Runi's... Wrong... ness.'"

Lena doesn't laugh at the self-deprecation. Instead, she picks up a knot of noodles and bounces it in the air. The cook's affect drive and clipped emotion could very well be in the same depot that Lena delivers out of. She imagines what it would be like to handle that cartridge, to step into that memory. And then the thought feels like trespass, and she physically flinches from it. She glances up at the woman. "You'd restore it?"

"I could. It costs a ridiculous amount to keep in storage, so I don't know why I'm still paying. Just money down the drain." Runi picks up her chopsticks again. She suspends them in the air over her bowl, then taps their ends against her lips. "And why store it, anyway? Does anyone actually restore these things? I'm not sure who I'd be if I did. Or what it would drag in with it." She looks sideways at Lena. "Do you clip much? You seem so collected. You must. Or are you just this perfect calm all the time? The model citizen Halcyon films in all their commercials?"

Lena scoffs, ignoring the last comments. "I've clipped. Routine bits," she says quickly. "Stress. Noise. Little adjustments here and there."

"Nothing big?"

Lena's noodles dip back into the broth, uneaten. "Nothing like that." Her throat dries.

Runi observes her a fraction too long, then lets the moment pass with a small, uneven smile. "Lucky you." She points her utensils at Lena's bowl. "Now eat. Before that turns to sludge."

With the instruction, Lena scoops again at the noodles. They've gone a bit too soft and the broth is salty and familiar, a distant cousin of the real thing. Warmth spreads across her tongue and nests briefly inside her. It doesn't go far, or last long, but it's more than nothing. And without forcing conversation, she and Runi eat. Lena doesn't mind the silence. Somewhere outside, a truck splashes through a patch of water and keeps going. A gust of wind shudders the window, a reminder of an outside world, but the shared space here steadies her.

When they're both finished, Runi reaches out to Lena's bowl, but Lena lifts her hand slightly, resting her fingers against the rim. She isn't sure why she does it—only that she's not ready for the small ritual to conclude. Runi pauses, but doesn't question. She takes her own bowl instead and places it in the sink.

"Thank you," she says, back turned. "For stopping. For getting drenched on my account."

"I was already drenched."

"Even so." Runi leans against the countertop, giving Lena the same careful attention she would a simmering pot. "You've been different lately."

Tension creeps back in. "Different how?"

"Oh, not in a bad way. This is nice—talking with you more. I like this other side of you, but there's this intensity… Like you're listening hard for something and don't want to admit it." Runi hitches a shoulder. "Maybe it's just the season. Weather does that to some people. It sinks in. Makes us reflective. Old bones, old memories."

Lena doesn't trust what might come out if she opens her mouth, so she keeps quiet. Another gust lashes rain against the glass, and they both glance toward the window at the same time.

Turning away first, Runi pushes away from the edge and sighs. "This storm might get worse before it tires itself out, and I don't think anyone's risking a visit today. You should probably get going; I think I'll be able to manage. I really don't want to get you in trouble. Keep your bosses content so you can keep visiting this kitchen."

The road is still flooded, but the water level does seem a tad lower than before. And as if on cue, her armband buzzes. Her handheld is probably angry with notifications as well. Efficiency demands attention.

"It's no problem. I can stay a bit longer," she says, hiking her feet up onto the stool's foothold. Her shoes are still wet, but Lena's warmed from the effort, the food, and the conversation. The notion of going back into the downpour scrapes at her. Being here with someone else, that nearness, feels better than it should—something akin to shelter. More than that.

Runi nods like that answer satisfies something in itself. She wipes down the counter again, even though it's already clean. "Okay," she quietly answers with another smile.

Lena settles back on the stool as Runi's hands move in

easy arcs. She cradles the empty bowl out of habit, one thumb rubbing the coarse edge and texture of the notch. She lets herself sit with the comfort and strangely, conflictingly, the growing unease—an awareness that something inside her is shifting.

Outside, the rain strengthens. But inside, the light holds.

EIGHT

Buoyed by the day before, Lena arrives with a steady footing. But the depot feels off the moment she walks in. Not louder or busier, just unusually contained, as though the building is listening to its own intents and devices. Everyone else on her commute behaved the way they always do. *She's* the one out of step.

But not in a way that feels particularly bad.

At the intake counter, Mr. Peng waits, stylus balanced between his fingers like a verdict about to drop. He doesn't acknowledge her until she's closer.

"Good morning," she says.

He turns his tablet toward her. Two red markers in yesterday's log. "You returned two undelivered drives. No accompanying notes. No route justification."

Lena's pulse skips. "I… The storm flooded the lower lanes. I had to reroute—"

"It was a shorter schedule. You had plenty of leeway.

Not to mention your stationary times; they far exceed the allowable margin."

The numbers stand on their own. There's nothing remotely clever or ingenious that Lena can offer against that, and the silence between them confirms it.

Mr. Peng repositions his glasses with a small upward motion. "Ms. Li, this is a formal warning."

It's the second one in six months. A strike against her personnel file. She's been in this position before, and she knows it's not a good thing. It's a different assignment, but the same cusp of dread. Lena absorbs the force of the reprimand. It should make her stomach drop, but somehow the calm from yesterday lingers under the surface like a support, bolstering her.

Mr. Peng hesitates when Lena doesn't move, doesn't say anything. He then adds in a slightly gentler tone, "You know what another one means. Halcyon won't keep you in this assignment. They'll move you out of the chain."

The concern grazes her attention. Another warning by itself wouldn't be alarming, but in this close proximity, it could escalate to a third strike. A third strike and this job goes. She understands that, even if it doesn't impact as hard as it should. Lena's already gone through one demotion. Where do they send her after that? Halcyon's known to find a slot for people willing to work, even if it has nothing to do with what they trained for. But when does that generosity and patience end? The implication ought to rattle her more.

For a moment, Mr. Peng seems to be on the verge of saying more; instead, he raps the input pen, then turns the tablet her way again. "I've had another courier take your drives from yesterday, and I'm shortening your schedule today. Upper and middle districts only, then go to the clinic and get balanced." He brackets his device against the counter's edge. "And take the depot car."

Lena's stomach lurches. "My bicycle is fine."

"You shouldn't be near the floods today, and I don't want you detoured again." His voice flattens. "Just take the car. It's the safer bet."

The overhead fluorescents flicker, and a jolt snaps down her spine. Her heart picks up and her lungs seem to compress. Aware of her surroundings and her supervisor's stare, Lena curls her fingers into her palm, trying to slow her respirations. She doesn't quite manage.

"I'll be careful. Yesterday was a fluke. My times are good." The words stammer out.

"Ms. Li, this is not optional."

The pressure between her ears and chest ratchets higher. Around her, the depot skews like it's being stretched and compressed. Lena locks her jaw and pulls a measured breath, holding herself together until the distortion eases. "I'll do it. I'll manage," she forces out. "Sir, I promise."

Mr. Peng squints at her.

For a moment, her pulse beats loud in her ears, the faint tremor in her hands slipping loose.

Then, unexpectedly, he glances at his wristwatch and relents with a frown. "No delays. And stay off the waterfront lanes. Log everything. No improvising." He points at the arranged sleeves and walks off.

Lena's rattled but relieved. Checking every seal twice, she works through the drives, then loads them into the case. Her fingers are still shaking when she shoulders her bag. She heads for the exit, not trusting herself to stay any longer.

Outside, her bike rolls smoothly under her grip. This is consistent. Efficient. *She's* efficient, she reminds herself. She repeats it again although she's not sure what the word means anymore.

The first push on the pedals wobbles.

The morning breaks into manageable sections. Deliveries go quickly and Lena keeps to the curve along the hill instead of dropping toward swollen drains. Her legs chug in rhythm along the taxing grade, and she enjoys the sparse traffic. It's like the city's inhabitants expect the storm to circle back and have stayed in.

After the third stop, Lena checks her device for the next address. She stops pedaling, coasting with the chill against her face.

Halcyon Balance Center – District 3

She reads it twice, then once more. An unreasoning sparks in her. Her foot slips off a pedal when she pushes harder than she means to. Her speed increases, tires hissing through shallow runoff, and the street unfolds in a sequence of familiar turns. Each block she clears sharpens the anticipation.

There, Lena parks her bike and steps inside the clinic

lobby. Mid-shift sounds mumble around her—soft footsteps on vinyl, plumbing in the walls, and a restocked cart somewhere down the hall. The space holds that citrus cleaner the janitorial staff insist on.

Soichi slouches behind the service desk, eyes half-tired, half-amused. "You again," he says, straightening. "I was beginning to think you'd forgotten we exist."

"It's only been a few days..." Actually, Lena isn't sure. Her sense of the week has slipped.

He laughs in a burst that warmly startles her. "Fair. What dragged you in? Or—" He partially stands and his eyes drop to the courier bag. "No. Let me guess. I am being blessed with official cargo."

She removes the sleeve from the case and slides it across.

He scans the code, and his expression shifts with a pinch of his brows. His eyes widen and brighten. "Wait." He takes the sleeve and turns it around, although Lena isn't sure what exactly he's searching for. It's the same as every other drive she's delivered.

"Wait, wait, wait—this is it. And you're the one bringing it? What service and fate!"

Lena's stomach clenches. "The counterpart?" she whispers. She would've never spared this drive another thought. It isn't the same old-generation model as the first one.

"Mm-hm." Soichi sets the cartridge back down. "It *was* marked for disposal, by the way. I don't think it's spoiled —just timing."

"How did you find it?"

"Didn't I tell you? I work miracles." He snorts. "It

was actually not *too* tricky. Old stuff like this has been copied over. *Your* file hit the queue too close to the monthly purge window, but somehow this one was delayed. Possibly just a cutoff limit." He leans in and whispers. "So I don't feel as bad requisitioning it here." He sits back. "This is the criminal influence you have on me."

Lena only stands there. Her body, arms, hands, and fingers want to stretch over the counter toward the drive. She'd been carrying it and didn't know the prize she had.

"You can come back later," Soichi says. "After your shift. I'll message."

She shakes herself out of her stupor, starts to answer, stops, and tries again. "I—yes. After my shift."

"Good. Now move along. Shoo. You're clogging this long queue." He flicks his wrist.

It's Soichi's usual humor, but the waiting room *has* filled more than she realized. Lena glances back at the service desk although the drive is already tucked away, waiting for her return.

The afternoon passes with growing impatience now that there's a fixed end. A clear destination. An objective she can hold onto that impacts more than just the end of another work day. Each completed stop clears another entry from her route. The tension of Mr. Peng's warning eases, not gone, but pushed to the side. Addresses and deliveries fall into order without much effort, and the scanners read on the first try. Her focus stays where it should.

By the time she docks her final sleeve in its designated locker, she's early on her schedule. Though Lena's world has narrowed to the counterpart drive, she knows if she goes directly to the clinic, her presence might draw more questions. She's not sure from who exactly, but after this morning's reprimand and the knowledge that she's pursuing something that isn't aboveboard...

She could clip while she's there maybe, process her maintenance balance as Mr. Peng mentioned, but why would she? Barring the disappointment of not finding the drive's cōng yóu bǐng stall, she's felt more alive in the past days. Sure, she's slipped professionally with her strike, but none of these ensuing feelings are unwelcome. *She* doesn't think so, at least.

Lena fastens the courier bag around the empty case and swings back onto her saddle. The gray ceiling of weather stains deeper, hinting at more rain, but she doesn't reroute toward the clinic or home—not yet at least. Instead, she angles toward the slope leading to the lower streets.

She has time. It's a detour, but she's completed her official Halcyon route. She tells herself she's checking the lanes for flooding, assessing the paths in advance of the next day's itinerary. And ahead, the water level has receded, but it's still deep enough to ward off pedestrians. Her shoes start to drench from the waves her tires spray up. As she turns onto the street, her stomach jumps, an uncertain rise.

However, it passes. Xiao Noodle House sits dark. The

metal shutter is rolled down behind the sandbags, a new row stacked that wasn't there before. A handwritten sign hangs off-kilter from strips of tape:

CLOSED — BACK SOON

No light or movement behind the slats.

Lena eases to a stop and the water shifts around her. She straddles and balances on the frame of the bicycle, suspended in time, waiting for the sign to magically change or the shutter to rattle or some other contradiction to the stillness.

No such thing happens.

Her gut drops like she's misjudged a step. She scoots the bike to the curb and stands there, socks wet and skin unhappy, hands tightening on the grips. In the lull, pieces surface. Words she's replayed since yesterday, things she wanted to say when the opening was there but she'd let pass. Runi spoke easily, shared so openly. Lena wants to answer that with something of her own, even if it's just a simple yes or no.

She stays there a moment longer. The block is quiet except for droplets tapping from a weary awning and a far-off thrum of generators. Lena reads the note once more, then adjusts her bag and turns in the other direction, her legs straining to get the bike going again.

The clinic remains. The drive waits.

By the time she returns to the white building, evening has laid a faint blue sheet across the street, and the glass along the facade catches the first flecks of neon from nearby signs. Soichi waits by the side door, arms crossed, one corner of his mouth already climbing. "Perfect timing. Get in before I remember I like being employed."

Despite his statement, Lena is confident it's his usual joking. His tone is easy. And like her multitude of warnings at the depot, she reminds herself that a reprimand rarely ends anyone, that Halcyon prefers to shuffle people long before they're cut loose. She's evidence of that.

She parks, unclips the courier bag from the back, and follows him inside. The lobby has been dimmed for closing and only the sconces near the inner intake booths glow with the softened amber the clinic uses after hours.

With a quick twist, Soichi locks the door. "Before you panic, no, I didn't tell anyone, and yes, this is absolutely against the rules, assuming your memory of protocol has faded. Shame on you. Congratulations on being a terrible influence."

"I didn't ask you to break rules."

Technically true.

"Please. You didn't need to." He flicks a hand in the air. "You handed me contraband while I was on official duty. That's basically entrapment."

She gives him a flat look, and he laughs.

"All right, all right, fine. Shit, *I'm* the one who requisitioned it. My name's on record." But Soichi doesn't sound concerned. He just motions her down the corridor like he's a soldier on a battlefield. "Come on. Before I lose my nerve."

He leads her past the empty booths toward the line of calibration bays—partitioned alcoves with sliding screens. They're nothing like the portable calibration kit above her desk. Everything here is clean and bright, updated equipment polished to a clinical sheen.

Soichi stops at the last nook, furthest back. "I prepped this one," he says. "If anyone asks, I'm resetting the reader for monthly maintenance."

Lena rolls her eyes. Who would she tell?

Inside, the bay barely leaves space for two. A single terminal rests on the small desk, its casing smooth and its interface newer than anything she's touched since her reassignment. But the layout remains familiar. The drive sits beside it, already unsleeved. It looks unremarkable. Plain casing. Standard seal. Nothing in its appearance should tug at her, but perhaps it's because she knows it's the counterpart to the defective drive that started this all that it *does* tug at her.

"You already checked it?" Lena asks, placing her courier bag outside the bay on the ground.

"Just ran diagnostics." Soichi leans against the bay frame. "Integrity's solid. Honestly cleaner than I figured, considering the original affect's age, and considering it's doomed for disposal."

Without asking, Lena slips past him and sits on the rolling stool. She braces her hands on both sides of the drive. Soichi squeezes in after her and the sliding partition closes with a soft track. The walls compress with its new occupants. It's meant for one technician cataloguing affect tags, not for two people about to break the rules.

Lena's pulse shifts faster. "You're staying?"

His shoulders pump once. "Is that all right? Unless you'd rather be alone? I can leave you to it."

Her tongue forms around an answer, but she stops and shakes her head fervently. Lena doesn't want to sit with this by herself, and if company—trusted company is offered, she surely won't refuse. "No, stay. You really want to see this?"

"Feels wrong not to after what you described before. Happiness? Food? Why wouldn't I?" He stands close, and although Lena's never liked having her space crowded and has always been particular about who enters her personal bubble, there's something about the nearness that she isn't opposed to. Especially now.

Soichi reaches around her and starts the setup. No wires, no helmets, nothing elaborate, just a conductive sensor pasted across the back of her hand and a contact strip placed where she can rest the same palm. The terminal handles the rest: pulse reading, neural tuning, and further configuration. Her kit at home could never touch half of this capability.

"Ready?" he asks.

Yes.

No.

Maybe. She isn't sure.

"Yes," she finally says.

"Go ahead then."

Lena touches the drive, its surface cool and unreadable. She slots it into the reader, and the designated screen wakes with a low-pitched trill, brightening as metadata climbs its display.

"Do you remember how to do this?" Soichi whispers although there's no one around them.

Lena nods hesitantly. It's not that she's never done exactly *this* before—what they're about to intentionally access is prohibited, of course—but even if she had clipped after her demotion, it's not like her years as an Affect Technician have vanished because she moved to courier work. The process sits in her muscles and memory, even if the stronger emotions from before her last clipping are gone.

Lena navigates the menu, checking the parameters, while Soichi adjusts the secondary pad for himself next to her. When he's done, her finger hovers over the first command. The booth goes quiet.

"Last chance," Soichi mumbles.

Lena's not sure who he's saying it to. When he offers nothing more, Lena selects the option and the next window comes up. A warning. Soichi audibly gulps behind her, but doesn't speak. She inputs the confirmation, then sets her hand on the contact strip. The system spools, and for a moment, Lena imagines it shutting down, the clinic lights turning up, and Halcyon authorities descending upon them.

But then a confirmation tone sounds.

The screen shifts.

At first, nothing, only a dim wash of blue light as the system links.

Then—

Heat against her palms. A crackle of sound in her

ears. A rush unfurls behind her ribs as the bay, the clinic, even Soichi next to her seem to disappear. Lena sharply inhales. She can't tell where her own reaction ends and the drive's contents begin, but she doesn't break contact.

Fragments of memory rise. Not cleanly, not with the clearness of images and sensation, not even the delayed but overflowing joy from the first drive, but slow and murky, as if dragged from a deeper layer. Hot oil. A counter. Steam ghosting into the air. A voice calling an order. It's the same. The scallion pancake stall is there, then abruptly eclipsed by—

Cold asphalt. Wet fabric. A hollowness so immediate her breath stumbles. It's like a missing presence. Content cut out of the world with only the outline left.

And then the memory collapses.

The terminal dims.

Lena's hand trembles against the pad. She's not sure how much time has passed. A year, hours, mere seconds? Her throat locks and her vision swims. Without warning, a wave of nausea rips through her, violent enough she has to curl to brace her breath. She clamps her jaw and holds on.

She's forgotten there's another person with her until Soichi brushes against her, shuddering. She doesn't know how long they stay like that in the cramped bay.

Finally, he straightens and peels the sensor from his hand. "Lena?" His voice has lost all its lightness. "You with me? Are you all right?"

They're simple questions, but she can't answer. She doesn't know *how* to answer. The feeling is too bare and too deep. It's grief without its story, ache without its name, a wound without the memory that made it.

What she's just experienced isn't the other half of joy. It's not even anger or fear or something customers normally process in the other wing of the building. What Lena felt was the absolute void where joy or anger or fear once lived.

She wasn't prepared for this. And worse, she knows, with a strange clarity now, that what's risen in her did not come from this drive alone.

Still beside her, Soichi lets out a shaky breath. "That was...not what I expected."

An understatement.

Lena eases her clammy palm from the pad and peels the strip off the back of her hand. She can't articulate it, but she feels...split open.

Soichi bends over so his head is parallel to the table, closer to her line of sight. He attempts a crooked grin. "Well. That was cheerful."

It falls flat.

His mouth softens. "Do you want to talk?"

"No," she says at once.

He takes a breath and slides open the partition. "All right."

He eases out and Lena stands. Her legs hold, but there's distance in them, as if she's borrowed her limbs from someone else. The first step out of the booth nearly folds, a misfire between intent and movement, but she catches herself before Soichi can.

After that, she can't be certain her feet are doing anything at all. Only that the space shifts. There's no seam, no real transition between bay and hall. Alcoves slide past. Clinic lamps drift overhead and light smears at the edges. Somewhere nearby, cooling equipment ticks on, oblivious. All the while, the ache finds her and stays. An absence and feeling she doesn't recognize closing around her, inside her.

She doesn't remember unlocking the side door, doesn't remember the air hitting her face. One moment she's inside, the next she isn't. And through it all, the world keeps passing around her, carrying her forward without ever feeling herself move.

NINE

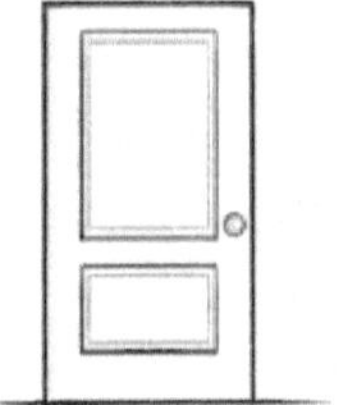

Sunlight filters through the narrow gap in the curtains and slices across her pillow, clear and unbothered, as if the storm never existed. For a while Lena keeps her body as stiff as a board, arms against her sides, hoping stillness alone might coax her breathing into an easier pattern.

It doesn't.

The air in the flat is wrong on her skin—heat smoldering high along her collarbone and a chill seeping into her fingers and toes. Her alarm rattles to life, bright and indifferent. She lets it run every tone in the sequence twice, then swipes her handheld silent. She stares at the ceiling, a spot, a blemish there she thought had been painted over. In the corner of her eye, a notification illuminates on the display. She turns her head, fixes on it until the display darkens. She stares at its blank screen, at the reflection of nothing, until her sternum threatens to burst. She still hasn't gotten her breathing right.

However, at some point, Lena manages just enough motion to articulate a message.

Sick today

It sends.

It's not true, except that it is.

She's lost. Nothing in her lines up.

Another buzz arrives, almost certainly from Mr. Peng. It's either an acknowledgment or a reprimand; both feel equally distant. Lena doesn't bother to look.

She stays in bed. By the time she registers the change in light—it's shifted now onto the wall—her neck and spine throb from lying in one position. Her throat is bone dry.

Lena pushes herself upright. Time has somehow slipped again, and the room, the flat, its noises, its lack of noises, is still unfamiliar and wrong. The space is narrower, as though she has somehow been entombed in someone else's morning and she's forgotten her own.

She forces her limbs into further motion, dragging herself into the kitchen. She faintly acknowledges her mug on the kitchen table and the sight of it, dirty and unwashed, has her reaching into the cupboard for a second one out of habit, but when her fingers brush porcelain, something punches hard and mean into her gut. Nausea rolls through her and she doubles over. It's like she's been hit by a truck. Her fingers curl back.

Wrong. It's all wrong.

She stays there a moment, hands gripping the sink and her head hanging low. The feeling of sickness fades but the misalignment lingers—worse, it burrows deep, deeper than a mug's touch should go.

Lena leaves the cabinet open, ignoring her parched throat. She drags on a jacket and leaves the flat. On the stairs she pitches her head forward, moving faster than the building deserves. On the second-floor landing, the floor tips. She catches the rail, steadies, then forces her feet to keep going.

At the bike rack, she stops short. She stares at the empty slot where her bicycle should be. It takes another beat before Lena remembers she left her only mode of transportation outside the clinic.

The clinic.

The counterpart drive.

That memory, and the yawning void that has not gone away, has only spread in her, swallowing everything.

Her stomach cramps. She should drink something. Hydrate. She steps onto the sidewalk instead.

Out here, the sun shows off. Roofs gleam as window panes shed the last clinging drops, and puddles reflect neat, bright copies of the blue sky. People meander with the relaxed pace that comes after bad weather, as if the island has been granted permission to breathe again.

Lena tries to fall into step, but every movement is off. If she was thinking straight, it'd be a wonder that she doesn't stumble or trip.

Neighborhood landmarks present themselves. She smells the bakery first, a sticky-sweetness before she has a visual of the actual shop. The pharmacy is next, too-bright with its harsh green lights. Down the street, a driver shouts. It's the same curb where she once got a flat and someone teased about her "professional upkeep." Each point should anchor her, but they hurt and are dulled simultaneously. It's all too much and too little, a juxtaposition that scrambles her being.

Pressure gathers behind Lena's eyes. She hooks her hands into her jacket pockets to hide the tremor beginning in her fingers, but she continues. The streets pinch together and buildings crowd closer. Avoiding the bright and cheery smiles of Halcyon billboards, she moves without counting blocks or turns. Sunlight angles across the pavement and shadows draw shorter. Commuter noise decreases, increases, then transforms in a different clatter.

Lena rounds a corner and stops. The place where a stall once stood is vacant. A few crates are stacked, the top ones leaning against the wall, a new addition since the last time she stood in the same spot. Likely a neighboring vendor's stock or temporary storage place now that there is no rain. Nothing about this space is wrong or remotely interesting per se, yet she can't move on. The corner was empty. Now the emptiness carries a pause, like it's caught between purposes. As if someone stepped away and hasn't yet come back.

Only when a voice announces itself and its owner skirts past does Lena move on. She doesn't go far, though. At the end of the row, she finds a waist-high ledge and sits. The sun's stored heat radiates through the concrete, and she loiters. A cart rattles past with boxes full of greens and herbs, and across the lane, two children chase each other around a convenience store's pillar while a vendor adjusts the angle of a cooler to claim more shade from the sun's reflected glare. The hour has slipped out of use. It's too late for breakfast stalls, and far too early for the night crowd. The market exists in its silhouette, idle and simply…between.

The plainness of its transitive state presses against Lena. She sits on the cusp as the quiet market and the busy city continue on around her, efficient and ordinary. Nothing here has been altered, but she knows that something important has slipped out of its track and refuses to return.

Her awareness turns inward, but it's all a mess. A vibration inside quivers and expands, a discord that won't resolve, and she's unsure how to stop it. It isn't painful, just…off. Like a string in her body has shifted out of tune, too slack to hold its pitch, but simultaneously drawn too tight, too sharp to the edge of snapping. For a moment, Lena considers curling forward again, as if the motion of physically bending might ease the effort of staying upright, the strange conflict winding and unwinding within her.

Eventually, Lena finds an iota of strength and pushes to her feet. She forces one foot after another, keeping her attention on the bare mechanics of movement. Heels set, weight shifts, the next step follows, and the walk back grows quieter. By the time she climbs the stairs to her flat, the sun has dipped lower. Her limbs are heavier than the day's effort and the incline warrants, each step up meeting some inner resistance.

Inside, nothing has changed: the small living area, the lone ceramic mug she still hasn't washed, the open cupboard above the sink, and the curtains left wide so the illumination from the Halcyon billboard pours in. Her bedroom is open down the hall and adjacent to it on the corner, the other door.

Pink.

Closed, as it always is.

Lena pauses, staying in the safe space offered by the kitchen. In this stretch of hallway, the chill is back, nipping at her hands. She hurries past, but at the frame of the pink door, her stomach drops. She freezes. A prickle rushes through her core, up to her shoulders, and down both arms, cresting and ebbing in the span of a breath.

Lena tries to draw in a measured inhale, but it catches. She tries again and it's as though she's sucking through a straw. She should move, just a few more steps into her own bedroom, but something has trapped her there. She sucks in again and shudders out an exhale. It's enough to unstick her feet, and she staggers back. She retreats to the living space and its small sofa. Her knees pull up and her fingers lace together around them. Halcyon's bright light shifts across the floor, and she stays there awhile.

TEN

Lena watches the Halcyon ad cycle again.
 And again.
 Ease, balance, clarity.
 None of it brings anything back.
 She doesn't leave the room.

ELEVEN

Lena's device lies facedown on the floor beside her, battery depleted. She isn't sure when the screen dimmed for good, only that she didn't intervene.

A stale heaviness clings to her skin with the encroaching sourness of sweat. She can register all of it, even if she hasn't acted on any of it. An empty glass sits nearby, and it reminds her of her tea from yesterday (or the day before) sitting untouched on the kitchen table. Its surface has probably dulled to a film.

Somehow, she's managed to return to her bedroom, after tiring of the Halcyon billboard looping its pastel reassurances. It'd offered its cheeriness and suggestions to seek support, to schedule adjustments, to "restore her balance." As if they could remove anything without taking too much. As if they hadn't already.

On her desk is the failing copy of the drive, its indicator guttering. Lena remembers the sequence and the shapes, but not the felicity or warmth that came with them. She nearly leaves it to die out, nearly lets it dissolve on its own.

But instead, she pries herself out of bed and inserts the copy, activating the calibration kit. The display stutters with outlines, trying to reassemble a whole from threads already frayed. Lena runs it again, knowing exactly what she's doing to it, and to herself. This is memory without anchor, motion without center, sound without source, and shadow without body. What shimmered days ago now breaks apart like paper left in water.

And even though the drive is only fragments—crumbs now—the emotion, the memories still aren't hers. They never were. But its collapse throws her own absence into sharper contrast. It's taken this long to recognize that.

Lena tries the playback again. It cuts out.

Some reflex inside her yearns toward a warmth she can now name. It's worse now because she *can* name it, knowing it's something she *cannot* summon. The shape of what should be there and isn't. She shoves the kit back and grips the desk's edge. The walls expand and the air is overly thick. Her room has been holding her in a slow boil, and she's only now noticing the heat.

It's too much. She claws at the chamber lid, ejects the drive, and hurls it out her open door at the closed pink one outside. It hits with a clank, bounces off, and drops somewhere beyond view.

Nothing inside her loosens. The void her outburst exposes only widens.

Lena grabs the kit, raises it above her head, but

pressure crushes her lungs even though the machine isn't too heavy. The pain spreads into her muscles and bones and she heaves a breath out. The unit drops to the ground with a thud and her body follows.

She looks away—shame rising—from the noticeable dent on the contraption's side, and her attention drags to the hallway, toward the closed door with its pink paint. How glaring and obvious it is now. A fixture she's let melt into her routine, a lifeless backdrop that is there in plain sight but had gone invisible in some form of object permanence until whatever this is now.

Lena forces herself up. Her toes press into the cool floor as she approaches the pink door, palm parallel but not yet touching. She doesn't know what she expects to feel beyond an anxious uncertainty. Fear, maybe. Guilt.

Nothing of that sort meets her. But somehow, the emptiness sharpens. Like she's reaching for an additional limb that's no longer there.

The metal knob chills her palm, and Lena stands there for a few seconds—or minutes. Each second—or minute—is a chance to reconsider and walk away.

She turns the handle and pushes forward, and the door opens without protest, releasing a breath that smells of dust and fabric left untouched for a year. Evening light casts a soft plane across the room, which has been preserved exactly as it was: a bed made with meticulous corners—so unlike her own messy nest—desk by the window, pale and patterned curtains still drawn back, and everything arranged in subdued order. Books rest in a stack that leans just a fraction, as if set down mid-thought. A jacket hangs over the closet handle—hers, though Mara always borrowed it without permission. It's the one that Lena never took back.

The bedroom somehow still feels lived in.

Lena's heart is pounding, but it's from her own anticipation of what's next. She holds her breath and steps inside.

Nothing strikes her. Nothing shatters.

What comes instead is almost worse.

It's not like with the defective drive or even the counterpart. Instead, memory surfaces in long, quiet layers. Not systematically like with a kit or terminal, not even violently, but in a slow, undeniable flood that seems to rise from a place deeper than the actual recollection. A hollow coalescing. It's not the shape of what should be there and isn't. It's *someone* who should be there and isn't.

A doubled laugh similar to her own. Two mugs, complete opposites in color, size, and style, gifted to one another, used for the first, second, third time, cooling on the kitchen counter. The garbled sound of her sister singing while brushing her teeth in the adjoining bathroom. A voice that is hers, but not. A face like hers, but obviously different to those who actually cared to look.

These memories have never been far. Or gone. Not in knowledge.

But Lena knows what's happened. Understood it at last. These moments have been emptied. They've been stripped of joy. Of grief. Of everything.

She recognizes each memory the way she always has,

or at least what she thinks is always—it's been roughly a year since clipping. A fall and a scrape at the playground turned into an embrace and ice cream. Fits of laughter at a silly joke made at their university graduation. Hugs and words of celebration on Mara's first day at the same institution in the office she wanted, and again on Lena's acceptance into Halcyon. An argument over their residence's mess resolved quickly by an impromptu late-night instant noodle snack. Every gossip session, every argument, every casual night-in hangout on the other's bed with a terrible soap opera playing in the background.

Every interaction reduced to a list. They're facts and records without a pulse.

Lena waits for something to rise. Her chest strains, searching for emotions that aren't there. Her body prepares for a sob, a seizing throat, a hitch in her breath, but there's no release. Lena's eyes burn from the attempt, not the emotion.

She takes another step, meaning to touch the desk or the bed, the dresser, but her knees buckle instead. She drops before she can choose to kneel, her body betraying her or accepting on its own that it's been carrying this deep-set deficit for longer than she ever allowed herself to notice. Her palms press into the rug, nails digging in.

Her sister is gone.

Her other half, gone. The joy, the anger, any sensation involved, as well. And in particular, the grief.

Lena did this to herself.

She stays there—long enough for the last of the light to fade into shadow, long enough that the tears come not from grief, but from physical strain—held together only by the residue of an emotion she can no longer grasp.

It's a paradox. Something that shouldn't happen. The hollow inside her contracts, taking on shape, density, and truth. Lena is missing a part of herself. And she mourns without the ability to mourn. The devastation is absolute, and wholly hers.

TWELVE

Lena wakes to the scent of old detergent, dust, and sun-bleached fabric. Even on the floor, cheek pressed to the rug, there are traces of her sister, and the blunt disconnection aches with the rest of her body.

From this angle, she's level with the underside of the bed. There are boxes now, but they dissolve in her memory. Her sister lies parallel to her, partially underneath the bed frame. She's laughing, trying to reach something in the depths of the other side.

Lena holds the specter there, unable to feel whatever she felt in that moment. Was it happiness? Was it irritation or frustration at her sister for losing one of her belongings yet again? It's so trivial. She reaches out, physically grasping, but her sister's gone and only the boxes stare back at her.

Lena shuffles back into the hall, slow and stiff. There, she can't bring herself to close the door. And in the kitchen, she reaches automatically for her mug, but it's still on the table, full of cold liquid with tea debris on its filmy surface. Her knuckles brush the handle of the other porcelain cup in the cabinet. This time, she stares up at its yellow shape speckled in petite blue, red, and orange flowers, but she doesn't take her sister's cup.

Two knocks break the stillness.

Lena seizes. "Mara?"

The name slips out as a breath. It's been a stranger for almost a year, but her tongue contours around the name like nothing's happened.

The tapping on the front door comes again.

Lena knows her sister is gone.

Outside on the landing something shuffles and then silence returns.

Lena waits for her breath to catch up, and she wills herself to open the door.

No one is there, but a tray sits at her feet. On it, a plate-covered bowl and a white porcelain spoon beside it. Lena squats and tips the cover aside. She peeks at the contents. Thick rice porridge, pale and full-bodied, dotted with dark-green cuts of preserved duck egg and slices of tender pork. *Pídàn shòu ròu zhōu.*[1] Not steaming, but still warm. The bowl's faded floral pattern marks it as Mrs. Kuan's.

Lena glances around the stairwell but doesn't cross the threshold of her flat. She carefully brings the tray inside. The zhōu still holds a gentle heat, releasing the scent of ginger and white pepper as she sets it on the table. She sits and takes in the dish: its sheen along the bumpy surface, the dark yolk chunks blending into the porridge, the pork treading, trying to stay afloat. Her hands have started to tremble and she places them flat on the table. Her fingers quiver when she guides the spoon to her mouth.

The porridge is mild and velvety, with ginger spreading in a gradual warmth. The preserved egg brings an earthy richness, and the pork a restrained saltiness that rises with its fat. The next spoonful dissolves on her tongue, and fraction by fraction, her shoulders ease with each bite.

When she's done, the spoon wobbles and tilts in the bowl. Lena lets the food comfort and anchor her in a way she didn't know she'd needed, although the emptied dish is poor company. Her gaze drifts to the second bedroom's open doorway and its pink finish. She knows that no one will come through it. Her focus follows the angle of the frame to the small indent, then to the trajectory of the duplicate drive on the ground.

Lena moves toward it. Crouches beside it.

The casing has split, small shards scattered across the floor, and its indicator light has gone dark. She takes a deep breath and with care, she gathers the larger fragments, and sweeps the smaller ones into a pile, scoops them into the garbage. The chassis of the drive remains where it is.

Lena doesn't stop there. Clothes, wrappers, the collapsed heap of the blanket in her bedroom follows in her tidying, piece by piece until the storm she's created and weathered is mostly cleared. She showers, letting the water run until the entire mirror fogs, then dries herself and dresses, fresh fabric soft against her skin. Despite the reset, a worn exhaustion persists low in her muscles, lighter than this morning, but still present.

She pauses at her sister's door, steps over what's left of the drive, and continues the short distance to the kitchen where she gently washes and dries the bowl, spoon, and dish. Lena busies herself until she has no other excuse.

When she leaves her flat, she takes a deep inhale. On the second-floor landing, her neighbor's door is open beyond the screen, and before she can reconsider, Lena lightly knocks on the frame.

"Sophie?" The shuffle of slippered feet, then Mrs. Kuan appears. She stands there blinking once, then twice.

"It's Lena, auntie."

Mrs. Kuan blinks again.

"From upstairs. Mara's sister."

A slow nod. "Of course, of course." A stronger nod. "I thought you were my daughter for a second, but never mind that."

Lena holds out the tray. "I wanted to return this. Thank you. I've washed everything."

Her neighbor pushes the screen out. "Hm. Come in, you look like you need more." She turns away, leaving Lena holding the door and the tray.

Inside, the flat is washed in the warm glow of a single floor lamp. Lena passes through the kitchen, and Mrs. Kuan flicks on the main light and busies herself at the refrigerator.

"You can put those there," Mrs. Kuan says, waving at the counter. She gestures toward the table in the living area. "Sit. Humor an old woman."

Lena obeys, setting the dishes next to the sink. She pads quietly past her neighbor, the accent table, and its framed photo, and takes the one open chair—stacks of boxes and magazines crowd the others. She rests her palm over the collage of photos and receipts beneath the plastic tablecloth, the surface giving a slight, clinging resistance against her skin.

"You didn't answer earlier," Mrs. Kuan says, fussing with a container and the microwave. "I climbed all the way up like a mountaineer! These legs still have life in them." She chuckles. "But down? That's an issue. I'm lucky I didn't break my hip! You would've found me lying there and it would've been a sight."

Lena traces a finger over one of the small photos of Mrs. Kuan's young children—possibly her neighbor's grandchildren, she can't tell. "I'm sorry, I haven't been… feeling well."

"Sick?" Mrs. Kuan makes a small, chiding noise. "I did tell you about the rain, didn't I? You didn't cover up, did you?"

"You did. I did."

"Mmm" is all the old woman answers back.

In the background, the microwave whirs. Lena's focus sweeps over the other photos and cuttings. Old prescriptions for medication under a name Lena doesn't know. A photo of Mrs. Kuan with a man, possibly decades ago, at the beach. She continues to scan this fragmented story of her neighbor until a scent floats toward her. It's leafy and warm, something heavier and denser than the zhōu Mrs. Kuan left for her. At the snips of cooking shears, Lena looks up.

The woman's back is still to her, but she somehow knows Lena's shift in attention. "I can give you more zhōu to take home—I've made far too much again. My husband always said I cook like there are a dozen people in the house." She snorts. "He might've been right. But you should try this. It's not in season, but my freezer is still full from the summer." Mrs. Kuan turns and brings a bowl over. "Here."

Inside the porcelain, dark-green leaves have been unwrapped to reveal a pyramid of glossy sticky rice, fragrant and steaming. The scent of soy sauce and bamboo leaves deepens. *Zòng zǐ.*[2]

Mrs. Kuan places a pair of chopsticks next to it. "Too hot? Blow on it, if you need." She removes the stack of items on the seat across from Lena, balances them precariously on top of another chair's existing tower, and sits.

"You don't want any?" Lena asks.

The woman leans back, pats her stomach. "I've already eaten enough. My belly is a balloon." Mrs. Kuan's gaze settles somewhere in the middle distance. "I used to leave out two bowls every night on the slow burner. Habit, I suppose. Mr. Kuan was always up before the sun. Ate his breakfast too fast, then complained he was hungry by nine." She tuts and shakes her head. "After he passed, I kept putting them out. And then I'd have to eat or throw it all if one of you didn't come by. Months! Didn't know why I was still doing it." She waves her hand and huffs. "So many other things, too. My daughter pointed it out when she last visited. 'Māmaaaa,' she'd say."

Mrs. Kuan goes quiet, and her mouth pinches. After a

moment, she folds her hands together. "Funny how the body remembers long before reason catches up."

Lena lowers her gaze, blows gently on the rice, and takes a bite. The rice is dense and chewy, the filling rich and savory, fatty pork and mushroom pressed into each grain.

"Sophie asked me once: 'Why do you not go to the clinic?' How could she tell me that? I was so upset." She firmly pats her shoulder as though beating away some joint ache. "You young kids. How can that be an option? Grief is earned. It's not something you can just take away. Not without losing everything else."

Lena chews through another portion. She stares at the spaces between the photos underneath the plastic.

"My daughter and son, they did it, and I was so mad. They didn't even tell me, just...packed away his things saying they were helping me. *Helping* me." She sighs. "Maybe that's why they've punished me." She presses her thumb into the heel of her palm. "My daughter, the worst choice she could make, moved off the island, away from me. My son is still around, though he barely calls these days. Busy, always busy. My children want efficiency. Clean lines, clean lives. No shadows."

The woman's eyes bear down on her.

"But there's no such thing as clean lines or lives. I've lived long enough to know shadows teach more than light."

Lena squeezes her chopsticks tighter.

"You haven't been out."

Lena continues scrutinizing the sticky rice.

"You don't have to tell me why. People go quiet and

stop moving when the heart is heavy. Nothing shameful in that." Mrs. Kuan leans across the table, not to touch Lena, but to nudge the bowl closer. "Grief is proof we care. Even when the mind loses pieces, the body remembers who mattered."

Lena swallows.

Mrs. Kuan sits back in her seat with a soft thump. She laces her fingers over her midsection. "But don't stay buried. Not forever. The people we miss don't return if we erase ourselves. And we can't do that to the people we still have here."

The woman's lips purse like she's about to impart something else—some specific truth—but Mrs. Kuan can't stay seated for long and gets another heated zòng zǐ, scooping it out of its layered leaves and into Lena's bowl without fanfare. "Eat more," she says. "You'll need your strength. Grief is heavy work."

And though hunger is gone from her, Lena eats. Mrs. Kuan talks, wandering through old summers and other stories. And around them, the space holds.

Lena knows she isn't okay—she knows that quite plainly—but sitting here across from someone who's lived her own losses and remained upright, the smallest filaments of steadiness return. It's not enough to lighten the weight or fill the hollow inside her, but it's enough to keep her from sinking. It's not a full relief. Just the sense that she can find her way back to okay again.

THIRTEEN

Lena reads the message twice. It's stiff, but it's all she can manage. She sends it and pockets her handheld. She doesn't wait for a reply.

Lena drags her fingers across the frame of her sister's open door, falling into the old motion without knowing when she'd stopped, and steps into the kitchen. She rinses the container from the leftovers Mrs. Kuan wouldn't let her refuse, then runs cloth over glass until it squeaks while she studies the horizon through the little window. The world's early blue holds with an almost artificial clarity.

Down the stairwell, she passes her neighbor's doors— both inner and outer are closed, unusual at this hour, but any alarm is extinguished by the scrawled note on a torn piece of paper jammed between the seam of the screen and lock. Lena reads it a second time, a smile creeping along her face.

She places the glassware on the mat, reconsiders, and positions it next to the tabled plant nearby. She slides a folded note of her own under the glass, penned earlier in her cramped hand.

> *Thank you for the meal and company.*
> *It helped more than you know.*
> *—Lena*

Outside, the empty slot where Lena's bicycle should be is like a missing tooth in an otherwise even row. She focuses on the sun's unintrusive warmth as she turns toward the main road. Pedestrians flow around her on the sidewalk, and the bustle of the morning commute has already picked up. Her pace is slower than the city's, but she continues with the faint sense of someone ambling alongside her.

She follows the scent of hot oil and sweetness to the next corner where a vendor props the lids open on bamboo steamers and sets out fresh *fàn tuán*,[1] stuffed glutinous rice rolls. Behind him, his wife fries *yóu tiáo*[2]— long, lightly salted dough sticks—in bubbling oil, turning them as they golden and puff up. Lena waits her turn, buys rolls and two cups of cold *dòu jiāng*.[3] She passes her handheld over their reader, collects the two bags, thanks the couple, and meanders on.

Her route winds through big avenues, cuts through quieter alleys with their mumbling cafés, and into a park on a small lot. It's not that she's never walked this way before, but now she takes in the old houses and buildings she's seen her entire life. She admires the new shops that have set up their wares in large displays. A circle of elderly men sit on benches outside, rocking and gesturing wrinkled hands at each other until one of their wives or neighbors waves a broom at them and they scatter. Lena absorbs it all without comment.

By the time she returns to the busier street, the morning rush is starting to thin. She walks into the familiar reception area of the Halcyon Balance Center. None of the handful of customers inside acknowledge her, but she observes them one by one: a man with graying hair in work slacks, dark rings under his eyes; a teenager in a school uniform twisting the hem of their jacket while the adult beside them scrolls through the newest handheld model; a woman barely younger than Lena staring at a Halcyon tablet as though it might offer her advice. Lena studies their faces with an unexpected tenderness. Words rise in the back of her throat, assurances she wishes had been there for her, but the door behind her opens and another patron taps his shoe against the tile. She steps aside, falling in as he moves toward the service desk.

Soichi greets the man, and when he rises to point the customer to the other side where the Restoration Practitioner's receptionist sits, he spots her, eyes brightening. The customer moves away, and Lena pauses before she steps forward.

"There you are. I was hoping you'd be back," he says, dropping his voice. "When another courier came by and when you never returned, I imagined every worst-case scenario. You never answered my messages!"

Lena grimaces. "I know, I'm sorry. I was—"

"Come back here," he cuts in, already buzzing the partition open. He glances over his shoulder. "Charlotte! Cover the front for me, I have to take a break!"

Just as Lena steps into the back, the same technician from before appears around the corner, a perplexed crease on her forehead. She mutters under her breath and trudges to the front.

"Thank you, Charlotte! You're my favorite!" Soichi says, words buoyant, as he takes Lena by her shoulders and steers her into the staff break room. It smells of ginger tea, over-extracted coffee, and chemical citrus wipes. The water filtration system whirs in the kitchenette.

"I lied. *You're* my favorite," Soichi says.

Before Lena can speak, he pulls her into a full embrace. At first, Lena keeps her arms pinned to her sides, bags thumping against her knees. But then she eases, leaning into the contact.

Soichi releases her and slides the door shut. "Before we get into anything else, just...are you all right?"

"I wasn't," Lena answers without dressing it up, "but I think I'm better today. Are you?"

He frowns. "I'd be lying if I said it didn't mess with me. I had an adjustment. Nothing drastic. I almost booked a deeper one, but I..." Soichi pauses. "I haven't felt like that in a long time. Or ever. And there was something about it that I...didn't want to get rid of, not yet. It's a bit morbid, but does that make sense?"

It does.

"Did you already come in for one? Clipping, I mean."

Lena shakes her head.

Soichi's jaw drops but he snaps it shut.

How can she explain? Where would she start? She avoids his eyes, focusing on controlling the slight tremor through her hands, faint but present. She raises the bags instead. "I brought breakfast."

"For me?"

Lena shrugs. "Yeah."

His face brightens. "See, this is why you're top rank of my ex-colleague list. It's a good thing I kept your bicycle and bag for you as well. You're welcome."

Lena smirks but says nothing. She sets the wrapped rice rolls and cups on the round table, and Soichi claims one of each and sits. Lena takes up her own. The roll has cooled, but the solidity of it in her hand, then the first bite—sticky rice, airy fried dough, pickled mustard greens, and stringy dried pork—fill the space between them as well as her stomach. The dòu jiāng goes down smooth, its nutty and earthy sweetness quenching.

"So, are you—" Soichi says around a mouthful. "Here to adjust?"

Lena wipes her fingers and wraps her mind around words she hasn't yet said aloud. "I don't think I will. That drive—both of them—brought something up." She gulps on air. "Something I clipped a while ago."

He slowly nods. He isn't surprised. "Before..."

Her demotion. Almost six months prior.

"I remember, I think," Soichi says. "Your process log backed up. Output timelines... I'm sorry, I tried to help."

"I know. And I don't know if I ever told you 'thank you,' so, thank you. Really. But no, I actually clipped well before then. I don't know, I guess it didn't take—well, I mean, the balance procedure took, but..." She can't fully explain why her work performance decreased after she completed the treatment. The grief was gone, but she'd still been affected. She's not sure it's something that science can easily explain.

And if Soichi has questions, he doesn't ask or pry. He patiently sips soy milk through the straw.

Lena's next breath clicks at its height. "It was... someone close. A year ago."

He waits.

"My sister."

Her other half.

The admission lands in the room with a definite weight. Lena could add more: the car accident, how ordinary the day had been until it wasn't, how she'd stood in this same room, same building, joking with him, before the call came. None of that crosses her lips. Saying the words 'my sister' already feels immense.

Soichi sets his cup down, and she waits for a quip or some Soichi-coded response, but he's quiet. He holds the silence open for her.

Her throat tightens and she pulls at her shirt collar. Lena went through with the Balance Treatment because the loss of her sister was drowning her. Because she couldn't get out of bed. She couldn't leave her room, couldn't draw breath around it. Because the only way out and up was to cut the overwhelming sadness loose. She hadn't grasped that the procedure would also shear away every exhilaration and every emotion tethered to her sister. And wasn't every emotion—no matter how small it seemed in the moment—still part of the whole? Still something that had shaped her?

And what had it amounted to? What had the clipping been for? Despite the treatment, her performance had still fallen off. She'd still withdrawn.

Lena sniffs and clears her throat. "You've clipped something, too."

"Yeah, I told you. When they transferred you."

"Don't joke."

"I'm not."

She studies his face. His cheek twitches up. He means it.

Warmth creeps up her neck.

"Oh. You mean what I mentioned before." Soichi chuffs, a sound close to a laugh but not quite. "I…grew up playing baseball—a lot of it—and I—" He gives a sly smile. "I was good. But my shoulder decided it hated me. No more pipeline to a league and no more contract. Losing that felt—felt like someone carved out my center. I was so angry and I had to clip it. It helped." He shrugs, then tips his head back. "I really loved the game."

"And do you now?" Lena asks.

His brows pinch together and he sits a little straighter. "I think so," he says slowly, gaze dropping to the side. "Huh."

Lena studies him, wondering if she wore the same expression at some point in her own wrestle with admission. Soichi seems to take it in stride.

"When I went through with the procedure," Lena

starts, "I don't think I fully understood. I didn't know what it would do to everything tied to…her."

Not just her emotions, but her identity and being.

"Would you restore it?" Soichi asks. "If you could. Knowing it comes with…all of that?"

"I think so," she says. "But I can't."

"What do you mean?"

She draws another breath and her chest constricts even as she exhales.

It takes a second before Soichi's face darkens and his shoulders depress. "You didn't archive it. You sold it."

"Worse." Her voice drains. "I chose full disposal. There's nothing to retrieve. There's no way to get it back."

Lena hopes for a second that maybe she's wrong, that Soichi can reassure her with some scientific contradiction.

But his mouth presses into a thin line. "No, there isn't."

She knew it, but the disappointment still takes hold.

"But," he adds, "human brains can be peculiar."

Lena gives him a crooked expression. He's trying to offer a flicker of possibility, something hopeful. They could pick apart the science, Halcyon's in-depth research and technologies, argue about how precise the process is, how little room there is for exceptions. That she might be an anomaly, that maybe some fragment of her emotions can be salvaged.

Instead, Lena thinks of her evening with Mrs. Kuan. Recovery doesn't always mean returning to an old self. Sometimes it's learning to inhabit the version left behind.

Lena loved Mara. She lost her sister. And then she

stripped the proof of that love and loss. There is no way to go back and reverse it, no reboot or even a duplicate file sitting on a shelf in a depot.

But it doesn't mean she can't try to feel again.

She walks home beside her bicycle, retracing her morning steps, guided by the unhurried pace and the after-feeling of sharing breakfast in a small break room. When Lena gets to her building, the sun sits high in the sky. She runs her finger over the groove in her handlebars and settles it into its stand.

Upstairs, her flat greets her with its usual quiet, though nothing feels as heavy as it did before. She doesn't stop, pulled straight to the open doorway. Her sister's.

Lena stands at the threshold. One breath, in, out, then another. This time she isn't bracing for impact. This time she's stepping in to occupy space.

And inside, the air tastes less of dust, more now of stored linen. The curtains bend the sunlight differently here, somehow warmer in tone. The bedspread lies exactly as it did the last day it was touched, a crease in the corner from where someone once sat. On the nightstand, books lean in an uneven stack—thin poetry collections, battered fiction, a few titles Lena recognizes from shopping trips she doesn't remember in detail. A sketchbook rests on top of another pile on the desk, a pen lodged inside, waiting for a hand that never returned.

She tentatively touches the dresser first, the wood worn under her skin. Then she moves to the books, picking up each one, flipping through and feeling their mass, thumbing dog-eared corners and the contour of familiarity, once imbued with an emotional record she can't reach.

Lena opens the sketchbook. The first drawing shows Meiyu's shoreline at dawn, ink capturing the curve of waves and the sun rising above the harbor. She doesn't know if this is an image drawn from memory or a sketch drawn in real time. She doesn't remember the outing if so, but the knot inside her loosens as she studies the strokes and shading. A sound escapes her, not quite a chuckle, not quite a sigh. Something in between.

Beneath the sketchbook lies a journal, its spine worn. The cover bends easily under her fingers, and she flips it open. Handwriting shifts across the pages, sometimes hurried, sometimes looping with care. Lena reads a few scattered sentences: a complaint about humidity, a note cataloguing which vendor has the best soy milk on the path home from the university, a scribbled sketch of a dumpling that is nothing like a dumpling, and an entry that makes her smile even though she has no recollection of the story it references.

An ache comes, but it doesn't crest. It doesn't tower over her, sitting lower and bearable. And the happiness she knows she had doesn't return. The grief doesn't, either. But another awareness forms. A sense of shape, a sense of presence, an understanding that even without the emotional record, the bond remains. It's an impression of a life that ran parallel to hers, an echo of a love that existed, proof that the connection is larger than its severed affect file.

Lena sits on the edge of the bed next to the corner with its little crease, Mara's journal open across her thighs. Her finger traces a loop of ink and the blotch where the pen once paused.

Lena isn't whole. But she isn't shattered. And as the afternoon sun sidles across the rug in slow stripes, she simply breathes and exists. She's present with what was, present with what remains, and present with what she can still choose. She stays, unwavering and calm, learning to rebuild where the despair once lived.

FOURTEEN

Lena pauses just before the bay door, her feet where the barrier of sandbags used to be. She centers herself before she crosses. Inside, the depot looks unchanged, yet the pattern has shifted. Two couriers wait by the intake counter, bags half-loaded. One Lena recognizes from another district, but the other is a new face, lacking the practiced economy of the job. He wrangles his armband, forehead creasing.

Mr. Peng stands outside his office, stylus poised above his tablet. He glances over the rim of his glasses as she approaches. For a second, the creases around his eyes melt then tighten, returning to their usual neutral state.

"Morning," he greets.

"Good morning," she answers.

"You're back."

She nods. "I am."

His device lowers and he takes her in, the way he always

has—measuring, assessing, noting details she probably doesn't know how to hide. "You were away for a while."

Lena grimaces. "I know. I'm sorry." She waits for the coming judgment.

But he sighs. "I wasn't sure if you'd come down with the flu, or worse, been in a terrible accident—I've been telling you that bike of yours..." Mr. Peng clears his throat and presses his spectacles higher on his nose. "I had to reassign your routes to neighboring districts."

Inefficiency. Mr. Peng's bane.

"I logged the days you missed as medical recovery."

Lena's exhale stops short. That's a surprise. "I'm sorry. And...thank you."

He tucks the tablet under his arm and removes his glasses, folding the arms together with care. "Your lack of notice and response was unacceptable."

"I know."

She waits for the rest, for the warning, the strike, the dismissal she's been expecting.

"I'll take your courier case and bag."

It's no surprise.

"I, uh, submitted your transfer request."

Lena blinks. "My what?"

"Unfortunately, it didn't go through. I'm...sorry. Halcyon's reassigning you to affect custodial work. You should receive your documents soon."

Her breath catches. He'd tried to transfer her? That wasn't necessarily a demotion. But whatever intent he'd had didn't matter with Halcyon's action.

"Hopefully your next assignment works out better

than this one did. I don't know the details," he says, dipping his head, "but I've heard people burn out. Affect Custodian turnover is quite high. I imagine emotional overexposure is common."

"Sir?"

"It should be quieter work, though. Less physical strain and shorter days. Perhaps it's better for whatever situation you're in. Make sure you pace and take care of yourself. Adjust and clip regularly."

Lena's brows furrow. *Is* this a demotion? She's not quite sure.

"You can make an appeal to Talent Management if you'd like," Mr. Peng adds.

"No. I mean, no, sir—this is—"

Lena had known about Halcyon's Restoration Practitioners, Affect Technicians like her previous job, the couriers, other roles, but she'd never given much thought to Affect Custodians. Between the start of her career and infrequent whispers here and there, she'd heard of this dreaded role. But no one really spared much attention to it, to the ones toiling away in some windowless and secure building, reviewing raw clipped emotions and cataloguing them before being sealed in their respective drives. For the island city of Meiyu, the concept of subjecting oneself to unfiltered negativity, even to experience short intervals from each drive—feelings, memories, sensory traces—is counterintuitive. Terrifying to most. A week prior, Lena would've felt the same, but now her heart rate picks up. Her eyes widen.

"I'm sorry," Mr. Peng says again.

"No, yes," Lena replies. "I think this'll do. I—I don't know what to say. Thank you."

Her supervisor—former supervisor now—carefully places his spectacles back on and blinks. If Mr. Peng's confused, he doesn't show it.

When the new courier drops a sleeve on the ground, he clears his throat and starts to move away. But then he stops and turns back. "Ms. Li, do I want to ask?"

It catches her off guard and she straightens. "I..." She considers, then shrugs. "Grief caught up to me, sir."

His expression hardly shifts, but he nods, and a rumble of acknowledgment comes from his throat. "Did you get it taken care of?"

Lena nods. Not in the way he's implying, but yes, she's in the process of what she believes she needs.

"For what it's worth," he says, "I understand more than you think."

Lena tilts her head to the side.

"I lost my Olive."

"Olive?"

"She was a beautiful beagle."

The unexpected not-truly-a-consequence consequence and this subsequent conversation still has Lena a bit stunned. She doesn't know how to respond.

"It was the practical choice," Mr. Peng adds pensively. "I couldn't sleep and it interfered with work, so I went to the clinic." He pauses for a second, and Lena's not sure if he's waiting for a response.

He isn't.

"I kept her leash. The leather's cracked, but it still smells the same." He smooths his cuffs. "Be safe, Ms. Li."

Lena thanks him again, her gratitude more full this time. When she leaves the depot, Old Man Hsieh is sitting in his security post, leaned back, fingers interlaced over his stomach the way he always does. His dented thermos is exactly where it normally rests. He glances over and gives his usual nod, and Lena returns it.

She mounts her bicycle, its balance a bit lighter now without the bag and case, and as she reaches the depot gate, her device vibrates against her chest. She stops to check it.

A message from Soichi flashes across the screen:

Joined a rec league. First practice is tomorrow night. Come by and watch my skills. You owe me boba after. Consider it payment for emotional damages.

A second message quickly follows. Just a winking face.

An unexpected laugh slips out, and Lena responds with a single word.

Deal.

Though the sign above the door is glowing, the skewed placard in the window announces the noodle shop's status. CLOSED. Lena disregards it and pushes the door, hoping it's unlocked. It gives, saving her an awkward entrance, and the chime breaks the morning hush.

Today, the place is different. Not only the aroma of

broth and ginger, but a richer nuttiness mingling with sesame, soy sauce, flour, and a hint of vinegar. Runi stands behind the counter, slicing scallions into narrow ribbons of green and white, and at the sound of the entryway, she startles. Recognition then relief flashes across her features followed by a wisp of hurt with the squinting of her eyes. Runi smooths her expression and returns her attention to her work.

"Hi," Lena says meekly. She's never actually greeted the shopkeeper out loud before; she's always moved straight to the back stool and counter space with a wave of a hand or an inclined chin.

The cook says nothing at first, but when she does, her voice is controlled. "You disappeared. Thought the storm maybe swept you away."

"I'm sorry. I've been..." Lena grits her teeth as she searches for the right shape of truth. "Off-balance."

Runi gives her a guarded look—caution woven in, although it falls and softens. "Are you okay?"

The instinct to say she's "fine" rises, but Lena pushes it away. "No," she speaks at last. "But it's okay."

Runi sets her knife aside. "Do you want to talk about it?"

Lena's shoulders relax. "I think I do, but first, if it's not a bother, I'm starving. I know it's early and you don't open for some time, but I didn't expect this morning to go —well, I guess I did, but then—no, never mind. I'm hoping..." She's not sure what exactly she expects anymore. She presses her fingers together. "Or I can come back. I didn't think this through."

"No," Runi says. "Stay. Unless... You don't have a

route to run?" She peers over the counter. "Where *is* your bag of emotional burden?"

Lena lets out a breath that borders on a chuckle. "Long story. I can explain later, if you want."

Runi tongues her cheek and watches Lena. This time, Lena doesn't shift under the focus.

"I do...want to know," the woman says. "If you feel up for sharing."

"Let's just say I wasn't spectacular at being efficient."

That earns her a genuine smile from Runi—unguarded and a little lopsided. "Efficiency is overrated."

Lena grins back. "And I've been reassigned."

"Oh. Oh?"

Lena only smiles wider at the woman's composed reaction.

"Is this why you've been..."

"No, I'm not sad about the transfer. It's a job—I'm lucky, actually."

She'd been ruminating over it the entire ride from the depot to Xiao Noodle House. Mr. Peng didn't call it a demotion—it probably *is* a demotion—but it doesn't feel like one to Lena. Not really. The idea of working with affect files, of sitting with unfiltered feelings, puts a strange lightness in her chest. She understands the burden they'll have. They won't be her own, but she's ready for the challenge. It isn't that she's trying to replace her own lost emotions, but rather that she's opening herself to something...close enough. Again. Especially now, with what she understands. And she has people to share it with, she thinks.

Runi's brow is still quirked, but the lines in her face

soften. "Ah, well, if you can, then stay. Come sit. I'll get your usual started. She reaches for the plastic packets on the shelf.

"Wait." Lena holds up a hand. "Not those."

Runi turns and narrows her eyes.

"You don't...even sell these, do you?"

"I mean, yes," Runi replies, feigning offense. "You've been eating them for months."

"But they're not on the menu."

The cook holds Lena's gaze, then exhales into a bright chuckle. "No, of course not. They're instant noodles! Why would they be? You can probably pick these up at the right corner store and eat them at home."

"Am I the only one?"

Runi places her hands on her hips. "Someone nicked a couple the other month, but that hardly counts, I guess."

Lena snorts. "Then why keep them here at all?"

"You like them."

It's a quick and simple answer.

"I don't know why, but you kept on ordering them."

Lena bites the inside of her bottom lip. She consumed the packet noodles because they were consistent. Predictable.

When Lena doesn't speak, Runi wipes her hands on her apron. "My niece left the whole box of those instant bricks here, and that day, the first time you came into the shop, you asked for one. You were in your headspace, and...it is what it is."

Lena bursts out laughing. She can't stop it. The story sounds completely outrageous but somehow entirely true. And Runi joins in.

"You have a beautiful smile," she says once it fades.

Lena wipes away a tear, and with the motion, tries to hide the heat climbing into her cheeks. She glances aside, but doesn't suppress the smile that follows.

"So, if not these dehydrated regrets," Runi continues without a missed beat, "what would you like? I'm a bit behind on prep. The broth's almost ready, but—"

"You're making something different?" Lena asks, glancing past her. A mixing bowl she hasn't seen before sits on the counter, flour dust at its rim. Bottles of vinegar and soy sauce stand open nearby, with small dishes lined up in a row.

"*Trying* something…old," Runi corrects. "But yes, I guess, different." She tilts the mixing bowl with one finger. "*Má jiàng miàn*.[1] After we talked the other day, I kept thinking about it. I haven't made it in years, and I'm sure it won't taste the way it did, but I thought…maybe it deserves another try." She hesitates. "Actually, do you… want to be the first? To try? How hungry are you? I'm almost done."

"For this, I can wait," Lena says, pulling out a stool. "I'd like to try it."

As she sits, a steadier feeling courses through her. She watches Runi work, the woman's movements confident but gentler than usual, as if she's giving the dish permission to become its own version rather than trying to force it to resemble what it once was. When Runi sets a small bowl in front of her, Lena has chopsticks ready. Runi bites her thumb and observes without comment.

The first trundle of noodles touches Lena's tongue and she bites down. The flavors open slowly: chilled and springy noodles wrapped in umami depth, sharp scallion, warm sesame, and the faintest sweetness submerged beneath the savory. It's nothing showy or dramatic, but it finds its way into her all the same, somehow calm and certain. Lena closes her eyes as she swallows. She lingers on the taste on her tongue.

"How is it?"

Lena opens her eyes and finds Runi's. "Have you tried it yourself?"

Runi plucks a strand from her mixing bowl, chews on it, and tilts her head. "Hm. It isn't what it used to be."

"Perhaps nothing ever is." Lena shrugs. "Doesn't mean it can't be good." And to solidify her point, she hurriedly takes another bite. "*This* is wonderful," she says around it.

Runi graces her with a wide smile, and Lena's face warms again. And while she eats, the cook moves on and sets up for the day's service.

"Hey, what ever happened with that cōng yóu bǐng you were hunting down?"

Lena shakes her head and wipes her mouth. "No luck."

"Ah, that's too bad."

"It's all right." She pauses for a moment as Runi chops the *suān cài*, mustard greens. "I think I was chasing the wrong thing."

Runi turns slightly at that.

Lena sets her chopsticks down, but her fingers hover, not quite releasing them. She separates the utensils, then pushes them back, flush again. She takes a deep and steadying breath.

"I'm a twin."

The admission and subsequent correction is difficult.

"Well, I *had* a twin."

Runi stops.

"She was older by nineteen minutes." Lena's throat works once. Twice. "For our whole lives, I was the younger one. And now, she'll stay that age, and I've… I'm one year older than her. Mara. I'll always be older now."

She swallows hard. "I clipped the feeling of losing her —I chose to destroy it—I believed silence was better than living with that kind of noise. I had no idea how empty it'd be—how 'quiet' is…it echoes so much louder." Lena pauses there, not because that's all there is—it isn't, far from it—but because the rest hasn't fully formed into more sentences she's ready to share. Not yet. But that's okay. When it does come, she'll know what to do.

The two talk for a while—Lena offering what little more she can, and Runi holding space for what she can't. Outside, footsteps pick up as the area busies and the lunch hour nears. A pair of regulars appear at the door, hovering until Runi apologizes, flips the sign to OPEN, and moves into the rhythm of service.

Lena stands to give space to other customers, but Runi motions for her to stay.

"Sit," she reassures. "You're not in the way."

So Lena does sit. When her nose, eyes, and stomach plead, she orders Runi's *niú ròu miàn*,[2] and this time she notices each part on its own terms—the broth deep and fragrant, steam rising with the warmth of ginger, garlic, scallions along with different spices and slow-cooked bone. The handmade noodles carry a springy chew, giving beneath her teeth before settling in with the broth's richness. The vegetables brighten everything, a clean tang cutting through the dish's darker flavors. The beef falls apart with the slightest pressure, strands separating, its long simmer coaxing them apart.

When the lunch rush thickens and the line at the door grows, Lena pays for her meal despite Runi's protests. She walks to the entrance, fingers brushing the doorframe, and the question forms without rehearsal. She calls out over the radio, enough to catch the owner's attention.

"Runi?"

From beyond the counter, the woman looks up, tucking hair back with her wrist. Daylight catches the tired edges of Runi's face, but also the openness within.

"What are you doing later?" Lena asks. "Would you… want to go to the night market with me?"

Maybe they'll find a stall with cōng yóu bǐng, and even if it doesn't stick around, they can still savor its flaky goodness, creating and building new emotions and memories. Or maybe they can find a different food or a different experience. It all feels bright with promise. The invitation hangs there, simple and full of something new.

ALL THAT HOLDS BETWEEN

ACKNOWLEDGMENTS

None of this would have been possible without my wife, who loves (certain) Taiwanese food as much as I do despite never having had it before meeting me. I love you.

A heaping serving of gratitude to my indie author friends: Irene Te, Ian Patterson, M.H. Cali, Stephanie Combs, Ian Young, and Katherine Kempf for their encouragement and feedback. Thank you as well to my early readers: Katie Price, Margaret Nguyen (my book doula), Holly T., and Christine Herrera. Special thanks to Jessica Liu, my go-to for all things Taiwan (and for reminiscing about making scallion pancakes with my grandma), and to Lee-Lynn Huang and Selena Kuo for their help with culture and food details. Thanks to my siblings, too? And as always, gratitude to my favorite proofreader, Brett Beckner, and my editor Erika Steeves.

To my parents: thank you for raising us in a strong Taiwanese community (even through my identity crisis years when I didn't want to be Asian). And thank you (and that community) for the Mandarin-Hokkien mashup I didn't realize I was speaking until senior year of college, when my Chinese-American friend looked at me in total confusion.*

---

* Though that might just be because my Chinese is terrible.

MENTIONED FOOD

TWO

1. 蔥油餅 [cōng yóu bǐng] – Scallion pancakes

THREE

1. 蛋餅 [dàn bǐng] – Egg crêpe

FIVE

1. 雞排 [jī pái] – Fried chicken cutlet
2. 奶茶 [nǎi chá] – Milk tea

SIX

1. 抓餅 [zhuā bǐng] – Flaky pancake
2. 大餅 [dà bǐng] – Sesame scallion bread
3. 滷肉飯 [lǔ ròu fàn] – Braised pork rice

TWELVE

1. 皮蛋瘦肉粥 [pídàn shòu ròu zhōu] – Century egg and pork congee
2. 粽子 [zòng zǐ] – Glutinous rice wrapped in bamboo leaf

THIRTEEN

1. 飯糰 [fàn tuán] – Stuffed sticky rice roll
2. 油條 [yóu tiáo] – Fried dough stick
3. 豆漿 [dòu jiāng] – Fresh soy milk

FOURTEEN

1. 麻醬面 [má jiàng miàn] – Sesame noodle
2. 牛肉麵 [niú ròu miàn] – Beef noodle soup

SCALLION PANCAKE RECIPE
蔥油餅 [CŌNG YÓU BǏNG]

I'll be direct with you. This is **NOT** a good recipe. Or really, this isn't a good set of *instructions* for making cōng yóu bǐng.

I learned it from the aunties when I was a kid, and to this day, when I make bǐng, it's hit or miss (either too salty or too little salt). The aunties never had a written recipe, and *I* don't follow a recipe. It's in the memory of my hands and childhood.

Ingredients

- All-Purpose Flour
- Salt
- Oil
- A LOT of chopped scallions
- Hot water (near boiling)

Instructions

1. Make the dough by mixing the flour and hot water in a bowl.[*]
2. Knead until it's good.[†]
3. Divide the dough into balls.
    - Cover with a clean, damp towel so it doesn't dry out while working.
4. Roll one ball into a thin oval sheet.
5. Brush oil on it.[‡]
6. Scatter chopped scallions across it. A lot.
7. Scatter salt across it. A lot.[§]
8. Roll up the sheet into a tight log. Squeeze and twist the roll to keep everything in.
9. Coil the roll into a spiral.
10. Flatten with a roller into a pancake shape.
11. Heat a skillet over medium heat with oil.[#]
12. Fry the pancake on each side until it's golden and crisp.
13. *Chiah-pn̄g!*

---

[*] Some people put salt in the dough mix as well.
[†] I really don't know measurements, I'm sorry. (Not actually sorry.)
[‡] I don't know what kind of oil, but I've used vegetable oil in the past.
[§] We love our sodium.
[#] Can be the same oil used on the pancake.

ABOUT THE AUTHOR

S.J. Lee is a first-generation American author with roots in Taiwan and Singapore. She is best known for her *Altered Earth* trilogy. As a security specialist in the foreign service, she has lived and worked in the United States, Iraq, Mexico, Chile, India, Brazil, and Guyana.

www.ingramcontent.com/pod-product-compliance
Lightning Source LLC
Chambersburg PA
CBHW031135130726
47988CB00006B/2386